"You know what they say about all work and no play, don't you?" a feminine voice asked

Michael blinked at where Kyra stood on the other side of his drafting table, sexy as all get-out. "I didn't know you were still here," he said.

She smiled, her gaze taking in the empty firm. "I could say the same of you."

Before he could ask why she was working late, Kyra pulled her shirt up over her head, her smile decidedly devilish. Michael heard the rasp of a zipper, then saw her shimmying out of her leather skirt, leaving her standing there wearing only her bra, panties and those naughty high heels he'd taken such a liking to lately.

She cleared her throat. "I've often fantasized about what it would be like to be stretched across your drafting table, having you work your magic on me instead of those blueprints."

Without a second thought, Michael swept his papers off the table and onto the floor. Then, with the adrenaline flooding his system, he boosted her onto the table.

Kyra gasped, her sexy laughter filling the room. "Are you sure it will hold me?"

"Sure. And if not," Michael murmured, bending to press his lips to her stomach, "we'll find out if these carpets are worth what we paid for them...."

Dear Reader,

Best friends to lovers. The best of both worlds, right? Only, sometimes the transition isn't as simple as it seems. And then sometimes it's better than anybody could have imagined....

Trendy architect Michael Romero already had it bad for his best friend, Kyra White. But when she transforms herself into a walking, talking fantasy, he can't keep his feelings under wraps any longer. Even if those feelings are not what Kyra expects. So, taking up his usual "best friend" role and catching her when she falls, Michael sets out to make her fall for him. The problem is, he ends up falling even harder....

We hope you enjoy Michael and Kyra's sexy, sassy journey into each other's beds and hearts. We'd love to hear what you think. Write to us at P.O. Box 12271, Toledo, OH 43612, or visit us on the Web at www.toricarrington.com, as well as www.temptationauthors.com for contest news. And be sure to keep your eyes peeled for our next Harlequin Blaze novel, *Every Move You Make*, available in September.

Wishing you love, romance and hot, steamy reading,

Lori & Tony Karayianni, aka Tori Carrington

Books by Tori Carrington

HARLEQUIN TEMPTATION
876—PRIVATE INVESTIGATIONS

HARLEQUIN BLAZE
15—YOU SEXY THING!
37—A STRANGER'S TOUCH

The Magnificent McCoy Men miniseries
740—LICENSE TO THRILL
776—THE P.I. WHO LOVED HER
789—FOR HER EYES ONLY

823—YOU ONLY LOVE ONCE
837—NEVER SAY NEVER AGAIN

SKIN DEEP
Tori Carrington

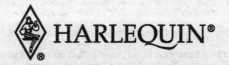

HARLEQUIN®

TORONTO • NEW YORK • LONDON
AMSTERDAM • PARIS • SYDNEY • HAMBURG
STOCKHOLM • ATHENS • TOKYO • MILAN • MADRID
PRAGUE • WARSAW • BUDAPEST • AUCKLAND

This one's for all of you
who have ever wondered "what if...."

ISBN 0-373-25990-5

SKIN DEEP

1

AW, HELL, what was it about her?

Michael Romero absently rubbed the back of his neck with his palm and eyed where Kyra White sat two tables away at the Tampa, Florida bar and grill frequented by employees of neighborhood businesses, including the architectural firm where he and Kyra both worked. Aside from being co-workers—he was one of four partners while she did the bookkeeping—they were best friends. A relationship that had been cemented when she'd first hired on at Fisher, Palmieri, Romero and Tanner four years ago. The first week on the job, she'd made a number of nervous mistakes and his partners had wanted to let her go. Instead, Michael had realized where the problem lay—her fear that she wouldn't live up to the job—and had befriended her. No big sacrifice. She'd turned out to be one hell of a bookkeeper. And the status of their relationship quickly escalated to them becoming best friends and led him to where he was right now. Essentially lusting after a woman who was off-limits to him.

Well, maybe "lusting" wasn't the word. But there was something about Kyra that jumped up and nipped him on the butt whenever he wasn't looking. Scratch that. Whenever he *was* looking at her, while she didn't have a clue about the direction of his thoughts. A strange kind of gravitational pull that made it virtually impossible to think about anything or anyone else.

Of course it didn't help that Kyra was sitting with the latest in a long line of short-term boyfriends, guys who would rate high on anyone's moron scale. His gaze skimmed over Kyra's long, shiny chestnut-brown hair, her oval green eyes, her clean, girl-next-store features, and her slender form beneath a long, loose-fitting khaki skirt and boxy white blouse. Funny, he never much thought about her in sexual terms whenever they were face-to-face, trying out a new restaurant, playing on the firm's softball team, or watching the latest video. Then she was his best friend, full of enthusiasm and challenging ideas, ready to laugh at his lamest jokes, constantly carping about his poor diet and his need for a woman deserving of him.

At times such as these, however, Michael wondered if the guy she was with knew how lucky he was that he could press his mouth against her soft pink one. Fan open her blouse to expose her elegant throat. And then, Michael pondered whether any of Kyra's boyfriends had a clue how to handle a woman like her. Touch her in just the right way. Stroke her slick heat until her breath came in quick gasps and her body tensed in climax.

Aw, hell.

Michael stared at jerk number— Hell, he'd lost count over the past four years, stopping at somewhere around number ten, though he suspected there had been a few more since then. Thirteen. He'd label this one Thirteen just because it felt right. Aside from being a very smug, up-and-coming attorney, Craig Holsom was attractive and he knew it. Kyra had been dating him for three weeks. A record even by her standards. Holsom's gaze wandered to a passing waitress, making no secret of his interest in the girl's generous physical assets. Michael stared down to his lap, where he was scratching his palm, and realized he was filled with the sudden urge to knock the grin straight from Holsom's face.

He grimaced, then took a long chug of his beer. He should have gone home instead of dropping by Lolita's for a brew with Kyra. Especially since he knew Kyra was meeting Craig. He was incapable of saying more than a semicordial hello to any of her dates before begging off with one excuse or another to settle at another table. Tonight's excuse had been a nonexistent date that was supposed to meet him there. It had become nonexistent as of two hours ago, when Jennifer Polasky had called him at work and told him she had to work late and was turning down his dinner invitation. She'd wanted a rain check, but Michael wasn't that interested and told her he'd call to reschedule sometime next week. He didn't bother to write a note to himself because he knew he wouldn't be contacting her.

Michael's mind ventured back to the object of his gaze. He'd already figured out that some of what he felt for Kyra stemmed from his need to protect her. He took great satisfaction in knowing that he knew her better than any other person alive—her sister Alannah aside—including all of the men she dated put together. He admired her strength when she'd told him she'd grown up in a two-room shack in a small town outside Memphis, Tennessee. He was equally as appalled when he'd learned she'd been working since she was ten, baby-sitting, pet walking, newspaper delivering, then graduating to fast-food joints so that she and her older sister Alannah could eke out a living after their parents had died. And he was even strangely proud that he'd been able to help her help herself when she'd flubbed up a receivables report and was almost dismissed from her job at the firm. Now she practically ran the place, keeping everything and everyone in line, proving to be the glue that held them all together when things got rough.

She was a breath of fresh air to a man who had grown up in a confused family environment. And she was a harsh taskmaster who refused to let him feel sorry for himself.

"Remember...things could always be worse," was one of her trademark sayings.

And she was living proof that they, indeed, could be.

But why she continued to prove the point by dating men who didn't have a clue about her true worth ceaselessly mystified him. Whenever he brought it up, she laughed, waved her slender hand, and told him that she was attracted to whichever guy she was attracted to, simple as that.

And Michael had been there to help pick her up whenever one of the jerks dumped her, as they all eventually did.

Kyra's face turned suddenly ashen. It was only then that Michael realized he'd been staring at her nonstop. He looked at Holsom, the way he held his hands, palms up, the elevated state of his brows as if explaining something Kyra wasn't equipped to handle.

Uh-oh.

Michael's fingers tightened on his beer bottle as Kyra reached out and rested a hand on Holsom's sleeve. Michael wished he hadn't sat so far away. If he were closer, he'd be able to listen in on what they were saying. Then again, he didn't have to hear the words to translate their meaning.

"I...don't understand," was written all over Kyra's pretty face.

Holsom plucked her hand from his forearm and put it down in front of her, then patted it patronizingly. The bottle in Michael's hand nearly shattered. "It's over," Jerk Number Thirteen mouthed.

Here we go again.

Michael started to get up from the table. It was getting a little old, this playing the knight-in-shining-armor bit. Especially since he never earned the princess's traditional gratitude.

Kyra urgently said something to Holsom and he coiled back, staggering to his own feet.

Double uh-oh.

Michael forced himself to leave his beer where it sat on the table and began to make his way toward his best friend.

But he was afraid he was too late.

"Oh, yeah?" Holsom said, his face turning an unappealing shade of purple. "Well you're about as lively in bed as a dead fish."

Oh, boy.

KYRA WAS CERTAIN her jaw was stuck in the open position. She gaped at Craig Holsom as if he had two heads. Which, at the moment, he did, because the room suddenly swam in front of her, not so much a fancy room in a trendy club, but the fish tank Craig had just plunged her into the middle of.

He was dumping her.

And he had just insulted her abilities in bed.

The problem was, Kyra wasn't sure what bothered her more. Sure, okay, when he'd said it was over between them a few minutes ago, she'd been unable to swallow the comment that their relationship could have been clocked on an egg timer...pretty much the same way sex with him had run. Then he'd gotten up and compared her to a dead fish in front of everyone.

Kyra let her eyes close and rubbed her temples. This couldn't be happening. Not on top of everything else that had happened today. First she'd awakened to hear her landlady pounding on the floor, complaining her alarm buzzer was too loud. Then during lunch hour, she found out the dry cleaner had lost nearly every piece of clothing she owned aside from what she had on. To top all that off, this afternoon she'd stumbled onto an accounting error at work that could mean her job if she didn't figure out what amounts she'd added up wrong and quick.

She'd considered opting out of drinks with Craig altogether, fearing what else fate had in store for her that day. Instead, she'd figured things couldn't get much worse.

Oh, how very wrong she'd been.

Quiet giggling from the club patrons penetrated Kyra's distracted state. She blinked and stared up at Craig who was wearing an all too satisfied expression on his face.

Kyra twisted her lips in contemplation. You know something? Michael was right. Craig was a jerk. The only problem was, Michael was always right. Which was infinitely irritating.

Out of the corner of her eye, she saw the man in question moving in her direction. Dear, sweet, solid Michael. Good. Because she'd need him to help her get out of here with at least a modicum of dignity.

Kyra pushed away from the intimate table for two, her knees wobbling so hard she was afraid she might knock over her chair. Thankfully, she didn't. She glanced at Michael's thunderous face, then at Holsom's smug expression, half tempted to let Michael have a go at her latest ex. But, strangely, she wasn't all that upset that Craig had broken things off with her. In fact, she was...relieved.

What did that mean?

It meant she should have walked away when he'd compared her skin to a peach at the produce section of the local supermarket three weeks ago. What a lame come-on line, she thought now. And about as original as the guy himself. The loser probably hung out at the supermarket to pick up chicks.

Kyra glanced around the club, realizing that almost every pair of eyes was on her, waiting for her response to Craig's comment.

She tilted her head and smiled at her ex, satisfied that he looked instantly afraid of what she might say. And he had good reason to be. "Yes, well, Craig, better a dead fish than a lost cause, even with Viagra."

She shoved her chair under the table, which in turn hit his chair, knocking the back of it against one of Craig's more strategic areas. He gasped and grabbed the vicinity in question with both hands, while one of Kyra's own hands went to cover her mouth.

"I'm so sorry," she said. "I didn't mean—"

She felt fingers on her arm. "Let's go," Michael said in that deep baritone that always commanded her attention.

"You bitch!" Craig said, probably meaning to shout the insult, though it came out as a high-pitched wimper. Even with her genuine remorse, she felt the voice fit.

Michael slowed his step, and this time Kyra found herself tugging him toward the door.

"Call her that again and you'll be eating your teeth," she heard Michael tell Craig.

Thankfully there were no more exchanges in the few moments it took them to get from the table to the door. Once outside, Kyra blinked against the setting sun, then collapsed against the closed door, the thick late-summer Florida heat seeming to spray beads of sweat all over her skin. She blinked up into Michael's glowering face. A lock of raven-black hair hung over his brow, his natural honey-colored skin looking darker yet in the waning light.

She glanced toward the door then found herself smiling. "I really didn't mean to...well, you know, hit him with the chair."

"That's a shame, seeing as it was so fitting."

She blinked and the side of Michael's mouth budged up in a grin. He really was devastatingly handsome when he grinned.

"Have I told you lately that you really know how to pick 'em?" he asked, rolling the sleeves of his crisp white shirt up his hair-peppered forearms while his brightly colored tie flapped in the warm breeze.

"Every chance you get."

"Yeah, well, I must not be telling you loudly enough." He jabbed a thumb toward the club. "Why you let morons like Holsom get the better of you, I'll never know."

"Who said he got the better of me?" Kyra quirked a brow at him. She pushed away from the door and began walking toward the parking lot where they'd parked their cars, hers a thirty-year-old Mustang convertible, his a rugged late-model SUV with two air-conditioning units.

With each step Kyra took, she felt any amusement still lingering from the encounter seep from her muscles. On any other occasion she might blame the reaction on the intense late-summer Florida heat. But she knew that wasn't the case now.

Her boyfriend had just broken up with her. Worse, he'd insulted her sexuality.

"Uh-oh. Here it comes. Phase two," Michael said quietly beside her.

Kyra elbowed him in the ribs. He caught her when she might have tripped over her own feet. "Shut up."

"Let's see. First there's amusement, because, well, let's admit it, a breakup between you and one of your boyfriends is always a source for humor."

"Glad you're enjoying yourself."

His grimace said the opposite was the case. "Then comes the grieving period. No matter how undeserving the jerk, you're always hurt by his rejection."

"Key word being rejection here, I think," she pointed out.

Michael stopped next to her Mustang, accepted her keys, then opened the door for her. She instantly pushed the button to release the ragtop and pushed it back.

"Then after that comes the eating. Week-long binges filled with all the stuff you gripe at me for eating."

She smiled at him. "As I recall, you do enjoy that phase."

He gave her a partial grin. "Yeah, maybe that part's not so bad."

She climbed in and he closed the door after her. She turned the key and the sound of vintage Heart instantly filled the humid air. He arched a brow and she turned the volume down.

"They don't deserve you, you know that?"

Kyra fastened her hair back with a ribbon she had draped around the rearview mirror. "I don't give you this much hell when you break up with one of your girlfriends."

He chuckled softly. "That's because I'm not the one in need of consolation. They are."

"Ah. I see." She scanned his dark features, feeling better just talking to him. "While I, on the other hand, am nothing but a heap of sobbing female hormones in need of mopping up from the floor."

"Uh-huh."

She smiled, but even as she did, a damnable tear slid down her lower lash and splashed onto her blouse. She rubbed at her cheek in irritation. She knew Craig Holsom didn't deserve a single look back. But she couldn't seem to help herself. Rejection was rejection, no matter how you looked at it.

Michael was right. She was an idiot. Although he'd never really come out and told her that.

"Hey," he said quietly, curving his fingers under her chin. "Are you going to be okay?"

She stuck her chin up in the air and sniffed. "Of course."

"Hmm." He brushed another tear from her cheek with a slow rub of his thumb. His gaze seemed to linger on her mouth, then he met her gaze. He gave her a coaxing grin. "You up for our normal postbreakup outing?"

"It's what I live for."

He narrowed his gaze at her, then tapped her visor to block the setting sunlight. "Follow me. I have a new place in mind."

Kyra watched him walk across the lot to his SUV. Tall, broad-shouldered and slender-waisted with thick dark hair and a grin that would look too naughty even in the bedroom, Michael Romero was drop-dead gorgeous. And he was her best friend.

He paused next to his car then half turned to look back at her pensively, his profile in shadow. Kyra caught her breath, then swallowed hard.

And he was her best friend...

MICHAEL LAID HIS HAND against Kyra's lower back and guided her inside the cozy little bookstore he'd found on the outskirts of town. The moment he'd spotted it, he'd known Kyra would love it. And he wasn't disappointed. Her quiet, wide-eyed pondering of the teetering shelves that covered nearly every inch of available space told him she'd forgotten the club, Holsom, and the breakup of a relationship that was bound for the Dumpster the instant it started.

"Oh-hh," she said quietly, as if they were in a library rather than a bookstore. "I love it."

He couldn't help grinning down at her. "I knew you would."

Her gaze darted from here to there then back again.

"Lead the way. I'm right behind you." He glanced at his watch. "But try to limit yourself to a half hour."

She groaned.

"Okay, forty-five minutes. Or I leave without you."

She smiled at him and kissed him on the cheek, igniting all sorts of interesting emotions he wasn't quick enough to deny. "You'd never leave without me."

He watched her disappear between the shelves and exhaled a long, even breath. Oh, she was right there.

He stepped in her wake, watching as she walked her fingers over the bindings of the mismatched, different-colored books lining the shelf at shoulder level. Her brown hair was still held back by that silly red ribbon she always wore when she drove with the top down. Which was all the time. Her skirt whooshed around her ankles as she walked. He silently cursed and called himself twelve kinds of a fool for continuing to act like Kyra's friend when more and more lately he wanted to claim her as his lover.

"Have you read this?" she asked, tipping a book out from the rest.

He shook his head. "Nope. Don't want to, either."

She smiled at him. "You don't know what you're missing."

His gaze leisurely skimmed her well-defined pink, unpainted lips. Oh, no. That was precisely the problem. He was afraid he knew exactly what he was missing. And it was beginning to drive him crazy.

He put his hand over hers and slid the book back into its slot. Her expression sobered and she flicked her wet tongue across her lips. Michael fought a groan and removed his hand, then continued down the aisle.

No, no, no. No matter how very tempting, he could never allow their relationship to cross over to an intimate level. He valued her friendship too much for that. And he'd seen firsthand that she wasn't very good at the dating game. He didn't think he could handle getting hot and heavy with Kyra only to say goodbye to her and their friendship in a few weeks' time.

Not a day went by that he didn't thank, and occasionally damn, fate that he'd been involved with someone else when they'd first met at the firm four years ago. If he and Jessica hadn't been going out, he probably would have made a play for Kyra. She probably would have gone for it. And the mess that would have ensued would, in all likelihood, have guaranteed not only that she would have left the firm, but also that he would have missed out on what had evolved into one of the most important relationships in his life.

As an only child, his mother from Peru, and his father from Spain, he spent a great deal of time trying to define exactly who he was. And if Kyra didn't help him in that quest, she at least insisted that he forget about that battle every now and again. And for that he would be eternally grateful. He was just him, she'd told him time and again. He wasn't accountable to anyone but himself. And that's exactly the way he felt. At least when he was with her.

Well, mostly when he was with her. Now he glanced

at his watch, wondering how far she'd go over the time limit he'd set. And just how in the hell he was going to get her out of there.

"TICK, TOCK," Michael said behind Kyra.

She glanced to find him tapping the face of his watch. She smiled then rounded a corner, absently running her fingertips along the spines of the books. She paused for a moment and took a deep breath. She loved everything about books. The way they sounded when you cracked them open. The scent of freshly milled paper. The varying textures, from the smooth glossy paperback covers with raised lettering to the puckered leather of hardbacks. The different artwork that depicted someone's vision of the characters or the topic inside. Fiction, nonfiction, commercial bestsellers, obscure literary tombs, the text between the covers didn't matter. She inhaled all of it with the passion of a long-time reader.

There were few things she liked better than losing herself in the pages of a sizzling, hot romance. Especially after having suffered a failed one of her own. Of course, Michael told her she was crazy for reading romance novels when her life already resembled an ongoing soap opera. "Stay tuned tomorrow for the next installment of 'The Days of Kyra White's Love Life.'"

She smiled as she found the romance section of the bookstore and began tipping out book after book.

Have it. Read it. Interesting but not up my alley right now. One by one, she scanned back-cover copy, took in the author name, eyed the artwork, then slid the books back into their neat little slots. One year Michael had given her a subscription to a book club for Christmas. She'd suspected he'd done it so he wouldn't have to accompany her on these book-buying expeditions. She'd maintained the subscription, but there was still something about the experience of buying a book in person that filled her with a deep sense of satisfaction. A feeling of joy. Of being surrounded by dozens and dozens of stories peopled with characters she could always identify with.

The sense of...well, not being alone.

She twisted her lips. Okay, so maybe Craig's breaking up with her did bother her more than she wanted to let on. But less than she would have suspected. What got to her was his comment on her sexual prowess. Or lack thereof. Was she really that bad in bed? Could that be one of the reasons why she got dumped so often? She made a face. Well, that might be the problem if she slept with even a moderate percentage of the guys she dated. But she didn't. The truth was she hadn't felt moved to.

She reached the end of the section and idly moved on to the next. Hmm. Still romance. But of the nonfiction variety. She pulled out a book entitled *Fifty Ways to Please Your Lover* and leafed through the contents. Her eyes widened at the graphic scenes depicted at the beginning of each chapter. *Okay.* She slowly slid the book back in and took out the next one.

Sex Kitten 101.

Before she could question her interest in it, Kyra absently opened the book to the index. Words such as "transformation," "new attitude" and "breaking old habits" leaped out at her, one after another. She thought of Michael's comparing her life to a soap opera. Pretty much of the same old, same old, with little variation.

She glanced up from the book and caught a reflection of herself in a multipaned window between the two bookcases opposite her. Outside the sun had totally set, so the glass threw her image back at her almost as cleanly as a mirror. Kyra swallowed, lifting a hand up to finger the silly ribbon in her hair, took in her long, straight brown hair, tugged at her oversize shirt. Plain. Simple. Direct. She'd consciously chosen the look because she thought it best depicted what she was all about. She glanced at the book in her hand, wondering if it was long past time for a change. And maybe this whole sex-kitten approach would be just the ticket.

She turned the book over and scanned the back-cover copy. "'Is your life based on reacting instead of acting?'" Kyra nodded. "'Tired of the same old person staring back at you in the mirror?'" *Oh, yes.* "'Want to shock those closest to you?'"

She leaned back so she could look down the aisle she'd come from. Michael stood there, frowning at a stretch of travel books, his dark hair tousled, his white shirt as crisp as ever, his slacks hugging his long thighs to perfection. She swallowed hard then straightened and looked back down at the book clutched in her hand. Michael would probably scoff at the purchase. A self-made man, he'd pulled himself up by the proverbial bootstraps with little help from his parents or anyone else. And, she supposed, so had she. But there was a big difference between being a bookkeeper and being a partner in a very successful architectural firm.

She ran her fingers over the cover of the book, questioning the wisdom of any sort of radical change. The truth was, despite her hit-and-run dating experiences, she really wasn't all that *experienced* when it came to the opposite sex.

Then again, it might be immensely gratifying to shock those closest to her. The image of Craig crawling back to her on his hands and knees begging for forgiveness certainly held a great deal of appeal. But for some reason, it was Michael's face she saw when she imagined herself doing anything with the information the author touted.

"'No risks. No prizes,'" she said softly.

"Done."

Michael glanced up from the travelogue on Central America he held and stared at where Kyra stood next to him, a glossy hardback book clutched in her hands.

"I think you set a record."

She tucked a stray strand of glossy brown hair that had escaped from the ribbon behind her ear, then shrugged. "It just kind of jumped out at me."

He reached for the book, surprised when she pulled it out of the way. He raised his brows. "What gives? You're usually eager to show me how literate you are and pester me to read whatever you chose."

"This one's just for me."

"Female porn?"

She laughed and moved past him, leaving the subtle scent of her perfume in her wake. He groaned and followed, his curiosity piqued.

"Come on." He leaned closer and whispered into her ear, "Let me see."

She shook her head. "Nope."

"You know I'm going to find out sooner or later. You might as well give up now."

She plopped the book cover down on the cashier's desk. He took out his wallet but she brushed him aside. "Not this time. Thanks."

Kyra never turned down a gift. Generous herself, they seemed to always be paying for each other's purchases. Neither of them had ever objected.

He crossed his arms and leaned against the counter, playing nonchalant. "Okay, I give up."

She eyed him, suspicion shadowing her large green eyes. "Uh-huh. Like I buy that one." She handed over the money, directing the bookstore owner to quickly bag the book. "It's not going to work."

Michael opened the door for her, then followed her outside. The sun had completely set, leaving a hazy glow around the street and parking-lot lights. The air was so thick you could have tripped over it.

He took her key, opened the door to the Mustang and handed her in just as he always did. He told her he was just being a gentleman. He knew it was because he always got a little glimpse of some prime leg as she climbed inside. Of course it helped that she was completely ignorant of his not-so-innocent game.

"So," he said, watching as she put the bag with the book on the passenger seat. "Do you feel better?"

She nodded. "Much. Thanks."

He glanced at his watch. "What do you feel up for? Some primo Cuban or seafood?"

She twisted her lips. "Actually, I'm not very hungry. I thought I'd just go home and call it an early night."

Michael narrowed his gaze. Talk about not so innocent. Kyra had to be one of the worst liars he'd ever met. Which, of course, was yet another reason why she was so endearing.

"Book that good, huh?"

Her laughter sounded unnaturally husky in the moist night air. "Go home and nuke something, Michael. I'll see you at work in the morning."

He hesitated then finally pushed away from where he was leaning on the door. "Okay. 'Night."

She grasped his hand, her skin remarkably hot.

He glanced at her.

"Thanks. You know, for this."

"What are friends for?"

"Hmm." She seemed to give him a once-over. "What, indeed?"

Then she started the Mustang and pulled away, not even giving him the little wave she normally did.

Michael rubbed his chin, then started walking toward his SUV. Why did he feel as though Kyra had just broken some sort of unspoken code between them? And why did he both dread and celebrate the possibility?

2

OKAY, something definitely was not right.

The following evening, Michael wove his SUV through rush-hour traffic, heat rising in waves from the sizzling asphalt, thick black storm clouds gathering on the horizon. He slammed on the brakes to avoid ramming a car that had cut him off from the front and prayed the guy riding his bumper wouldn't hit him from behind.

Michael blew out a long breath. Wrangling with traffic was not helping his dark mood.

He'd had an odd sensation in his gut ever since he'd watched Kyra drive off from the bookstore. And that feeling had only gained momentum since then. He'd gotten her answering machine when he'd called to check on her last night. And every time he'd ducked into her office throughout the day, she'd had her nose stuck in that book. She'd still refused to let him see it. And the paper bag she'd taped to the cover only lent a more mysterious quality to the hardback. Then when he'd stopped by her office to see if she wanted to go for a cup of coffee after work, he'd discovered she'd left an hour earlier.

What in the hell was the matter with her? Was she upset with him? She didn't seem to be. In fact, she didn't seem to be all that upset about Craig Holsom and their breakup, either. Which was odder still. It usually took her a good long week of moping, mock depression, and marathon eating to get over a breakup, even if the relationship itself had only lasted the same amount of time.

He just didn't get it.

An exit ramp emerged to his right, a new shopping complex beckoning him from beyond. He swerved to get off the crowded highway. Maybe he'd given up too easily last night. Maybe she'd needed him. Maybe he'd read the signals wrong and she'd spent the night washing her pillow with tears.

The thought made his jaw clench. Craig Holsom, and the dozen or so that had come before him, didn't deserve an hour of Kyra's company, much less a single one of her tears.

A pint of Ben & Jerry's. That should get Kyra to open up to him. Tell him what was going on. He quickly stopped by a nearby store, made the purchase, then pointed the SUV in the direction of her apartment complex. Within twenty minutes he stood on the second-floor landing, knocking on her door.

"Kyra?" he called through the old, neon-pink-painted door.

No response.

He grimaced. Her Mustang was parked at the curb, so he knew she had to be home. "I know you're in there, so you might as well open up."

Of course, there was the possibility that she'd already replaced Holsom with the next jerk on her list. The thought bothered him more than it should have. Far more.

He cursed under his breath and knocked again.

"Do you mind! Some people are trying to watch

Wheel of Fortune! Keep it down up there!'' the landlady who lived a floor below bellowed up the stairs. ''This ain't no bordello.''

Not that you could tell by her language, Michael thought. He stared down the winding stairwell right into Mrs. Kaminsky's too-thin, aging face. He always found it hard to believe that such a window-shattering voice could come from such a small package. ''Sorry, Mrs. K., I'll try to be more quiet.''

''You do that!'' she yelled, nearly blowing back his hair.

Michael grimaced and stepped up to Kyra's apartment door. Why Kyra put up with the old battle-ax was beyond him. Strangely, she seemed to like the landlady's interference. Perhaps because she'd had such little parental involvement for so much of her life.

''Kyra?'' he said more quietly, curving his hand around the doorknob. It turned easily. Figures she'd leave her door unlocked. Then again, he couldn't imagine any thief with the guts to get past Mrs. Kaminsky.

He pushed open the door and peered around the colorfully decorated interior of the apartment. The old place was nice. With large, airy rooms and polished pale wood floors, the one-bedroom apartment almost made putting up with the curmudgeonly old landlady worth it. Almost. If Michael were Kyra, he'd have moved out a long time ago.

''Kyra?'' He softly closed the door behind him, eyeing a line of discarded clothes littering the floor. He frowned and picked up the skirt she'd been wearing earlier. Kyra was fastidiously neat. It wasn't like her to just leave her clothes lying around... He picked up each item as he went, then peered into the empty bedroom. Where was she? His gaze focused on a small, empty box sitting just outside the closed bathroom door. Dropping the skirt, he picked up the box and knocked on the door.

"Kyra, are you in there?"

A small squeal told him that she was. He turned the box around. Hair dye? He grimaced. What in the hell was she doing in there?

The lock clicked on the door and he stepped back, expecting her to come out. He quickly discovered that she hadn't been unlocking the door, but rather locking it, as if afraid he would come in.

"Kyra, what the hell is going on?" he asked through the thick wood.

"Go away," she said.

Michael leaned against the doorjamb and sighed. "You're upset with me. That's it, isn't it? The reason why you didn't want to go out to eat with me last night, why you barely talked to me today."

"Don't be stupid."

He looked at where he still held the ice cream in his other hand and considered putting it in the freezer. "If I said something to make you angry with me, I apologize."

"No need to apologize."

"I see. Is that because there isn't anything to apologize for? Or are you saying I shouldn't waste my time because what I said or did was completely unforgivable?"

A soft giggle filtered through the wood. He stared at the door, wondering just what was so funny.

"Kyra, come on out here and talk to me. I'm not into talking to doors."

Silence.

Uh-oh. This was worse than he thought. And he was at a loss as to what to do next.

Not once in the past four years had he seen Kyra angry. In fact, he hadn't a clue what it looked like. Would she giggle if she was upset? He wouldn't discount the possibility.

Well, there had been that time when they were in a mall parking lot and a woman had dumped a kitten out of her car mere feet from a busy intersection. Kyra had rescued the scrap of fur—the feline in question that even now lazily considered Michael from his perch on top of the silent television—and given the woman what-for. He'd almost forgotten about the incident because it was so uncharacteristic for Kyra to lose her cool about anything. You wanted to cut in line? No problem. It probably meant you were in more of a hurry than she was. Heck, you might even have a wife in labor waiting in the car who wouldn't go to the hospital until you got her that case of beer. You honked your horn at her and she would wave at you, thinking the gesture a greeting rather than a rebuke.

Michael sighed and closed his eyes. There was no telling exactly what was going through Kyra's mind.

Suddenly the door opened inward, taking away Michael's leaning support and nearly toppling him to the floor.

"Give a guy some warning, why don't you," he mumbled, fighting to straighten himself.

Only once he was standing, he realized that the open door wasn't the only thing to knock him off balance. Kyra's appearance absolutely floored him.

"So?" KYRA ASKED, barely able to conceal her excitement as she forced herself to stand completely still in front of Michael. "What do you think?"

He stumbled backward a couple of steps, his mouth moving, although no sounds came out.

"I know. Something, isn't it? I hardly recognized myself in the mirror just now."

And she hardly had. Who knew what a difference two little hours could make in someone's life? Kyra reached up to pluck at her newly cropped hair, still feeling light-headed by the absence of the weight of her long tresses. But she hadn't stopped at the short, sassily styled 'do. Oh, no. On the way home from the salon she'd decided she'd wanted to change the color, as well, and picked up one of those home dye kits. She'd always been curious about the saying that blondes had more fun. She wanted to find out for herself if it was true.

Then, of course, there was her new wardrobe. Having to replace the things the cleaner had lost anyway, she'd gone shopping with the check they'd issued to cover the loss. But she'd stayed well away from the places where she usually bought her clothes. Instead she'd ventured into the trendy little shops in Ybor City and taken the advice of the salesgirls. The outfit she had on now was her favorite—a hot-pink stretchy tank top with a tight little mock-leopard-skin leather skirt.

True, so maybe she'd felt as if she was in little more than her underwear and wondering where the rest of her clothes were when she'd first tried the racy outfit on. But the more minutes that had ticked by, the more comfortable she'd felt. Not only in her new duds, but in her skin, period. And the new clothes helped her make one very important discovery—she had breasts! Sure, she'd always known she'd *had* them, had them. She just hadn't realized how round and smooth and sexy they were. Which was plausible because they were usually hidden under three layers of clothing and an unattractive slingshot of a bra.

Michael suddenly looked pale. Her smile vanished and she stepped forward, nearly tripping over the four-inch heels she wore. Okay, these would take a little getting used to. "Are you all right?" she asked, guiding him away from the plant stand that held her favorite fern and toward the couch. He plopped down onto the pale cushions as though his spine had disappeared, and sat there staring at her.

She giggled, the sound emerging foreign to her own ears. She didn't giggle. In fact, she didn't even think she knew how. "I know, isn't it something? The girl at the store told me hoseless was the way to go, but I think the fishnet stockings make the outfit. Don't you?"

"I—I—I—"

Kyra put her hands on her hips, liking the feel of her body beneath the sexy material. "You...?"

"I...brought you some ice cream," he croaked, thrusting a bag in her direction.

"Hmm, Half Baked, 2-Twisted. My favorite," she said. "But I'm afraid if I have any of it right now, I'll pop a seam or something."

"Or...or something," Michael agreed.

Walking on the tips of her toes, she stepped into the kitchen and put the ice cream in the freezer.

"So?" she prompted, standing in front of him again.

"So—" He cleared his throat. "So, what?"

She rolled her eyes to stare at the ceiling. "You didn't answer my question. What do you think?"

His dark eyes narrowed as he looked everywhere but at her.

"Oh, come on, Michael. Look at me."

"No."

His quick refusal made her laugh.

"It's like looking at my sister naked. If I had a sister. Which I don't. But seeing as..." His mouth clamped closed and he continued staring at the opposite wall.

"Not exactly the reaction I was hoping for."

His gaze slammed into hers. Kyra nearly stumbled backward from the impact. A heated question loomed large in his dark eyes as he considered her. A shiver ran over her skin like a lover's touch, heating her blood and making her nipples harden.

She shifted her weight from one foot to the other. "What's the matter? It's not like you haven't looked at me before. You've seen me in less than this plenty of times."

"Oh, yeah? When?"

"When we go to the beach, for starters."

"Oh."

She smiled.

"You're...you're..."

She gestured with her hand. "I'm..."

"Blond."

She sighed. "Trust you to state the obvious. For a guy who designs houses, you are completely unimaginative in your personal life, you know?"

"Yes, well, judging by the looks of you, you have enough imagination for both of us."

A reaction. Now they were talking.

"Do you think it's original? I mean, I just kind of went with my gut. Chose things I liked instead of what I thought would be appropriate." She shivered again, relishing the zing of daring rushing through her veins. She held up her hands. "Wait. Now that I finally have your attention, I want your complete opinion." Swiveling around on the heels a little too quickly, she teetered precariously, and reached for something to hold on to. There was nothing. She landed squarely in Michael's lap.

Air rushed from Kyra's lungs at the sudden move. She giggled and wriggled around to face him. And immediately became aware of a reaction she would never have thought she'd get from him.

"Oh," she murmured. "Oh!"

Talk about your shockers. Yes, she had expected to shock Michael. But she hadn't expected to be shocked by his...well, shock. She caught her breath, amazed that she had elicited such a reaction. And more than just a little thrilled....

OH, INDEED.

Awareness surged through Michael's bloodstream like an overpowering drug. Everything that was Kyra filled his senses. Her sweet smell. Her soft hair. Her even softer skin. Her slender, very voluptuous body.

Somehow, Michael managed to shift Kyra from where her bottom fit snuggly against his painful erection. But he stopped himself short of lifting her all the way off his lap. Truth was, he liked her right where she was, thank you very much. Even if it was only for a few precious moments.

And, God help him, he liked the changes she'd undergone. While he'd always been fascinated with her long, shiny brown hair, the short, blond curls suited her oval face and the warm-honey tone of her skin. And the cut somehow made her pink lips look all pouty and kissable. He'd never really realized how full her mouth was until that moment, watching with rapt attention as her wet tongue flicked across her bottom lip.

Aw, hell.

And the clothes...

Yes, while he had seen her in a bathing suit, her choice in swimming apparel had always been as unassuming as her choice in clothes. He'd always known she had a nice figure, but within a blink of an eye she'd gone from pleasingly attractive to va-va-voom hot.

And he'd give anything in the world to kiss her in that one moment.

Kiss her? Hell, he wanted to sink into her slick flesh and ram into her like nobody's business.

"Michael?"

He blinked and two very pert, very round breasts filled his line of sight. The pink material of her low-scooped tank hugged the mounds to perfection...and did little to hide her own reaction to their close proximity. Forget kissing her. He wanted to fasten his mouth around one of those engorged nipples. Scratch that. He wanted to swallow both of them at the same time.

Kyra wriggled, gaining his attention as her leather skirt slid against the smooth material of his slacks. He groaned and blinked again, bringing her face into focus.

She smiled at him. "I have breasts," she told him.

He nearly choked on his own saliva.

"I mean, of course I have breasts. We're all born with them. It's just that—" she looked down, considering the area he'd been drawn to mere moments before "—who knew a bra could do this?"

"Um, yeah, who knew," Michael agreed. She shimmied to straighten her top, and nearly pushed him right over the top. "Um, Kyra?" he said in low warning. "I think you'd better get up."

She blinked at him. Charcoal-black ringed her lashes, making the green of her eyes that much more mesmerizing. "Oh," she said, considering him. "Oh!"

Michael didn't know which was worse. Her realizing what kind of state he was in or her not responding in kind to that same reaction.

Kyra budged, finally pushing up from the couch and regaining her footing. Or as much of it as she was going to gain in those sexy, black stiletto...those ridiculous heels. Heels that made her legs look as if they went on forever. And that she would probably break her neck in if she tried to walk more than ten feet.

"So...you like?" she asked point-blank, propping a slender hand with purple-painted nails on a too curvy hip. Was that leopard skin?

"Um," he said, struggling to a better sitting position on the too soft couch. He didn't dare stand for fear that he might injure himself. "'Like'...isn't the word I'd use, exactly."

Was it him, or had suggestion just darkened her eyes?

"Then what is the word you'd use?"

Siren? Luscious? Hot? "Different," he said.

The cat lifted his head from his position on the television. Michael was sure that if Mr. Tibbs had been able to roll his eyes at him, he would have. He glared at the tom, and gestured vaguely toward Kyra.

"Is there any particular reason for your...this..."

"Transformation?"

He hiked his brows. Transformation? As in a permanent way of living? As in out with the old, in with the new?

As in there was no way in hell he was going to survive with her looking like that twenty-four/seven?

He gave a deep, loud mental groan. He couldn't handle two minutes with Kyra looking like that. How was he going to endure an entire friendship? "Um, that'll do."

She plucked up the clothing he'd dropped earlier, then swaggered toward the kitchen. Her gait was unsure, gutsy, making her look that much sexier. She opened the chrome garbage can and dropped the items inside, brushing her hands together as the lid closed.

She looked at him and he felt the urge to look away, as if merely meeting her eyes would reveal his true feelings.

"Does there have to be a reason? I mean, aside from my being long overdue for a reality check?" She twisted her lips. "I've lived twenty-four years looking like an old maid. It's about time I looked more like the women my age."

No woman your age looks like this, he wanted to tell her. But the words never made it past his lips. Sure, other women might dress that way, but not one of them could pull off the look the way Kyra did with so little or no effort. There was a quirky innocence, a playful charm, that made Kyra even sexier and impossible not to notice—as certain parts of his body could attest to. A curious naiveté and irresistible daring that made her look like one-third dressed-up teen, two-thirds single, professional female on the make.

Michael wanted to bang his hand against his head until it started working again. Until he stopped drooling after his best friend and started thinking with the parts of his body that mattered. Until he stopped wanting to throw her onto the couch behind him and explore those succulent breasts and plunge into her sweet-smelling flesh, those high heels piercing the air behind his back.

Instead he tugged on his shirt collar until he choked himself.

"Are you ready?" She struck a pose that was one-hundred-percent challenge. "It's time to go out to let the world know the new Kyra has arrived."

3

KYRA ACCIDENTALLY DROPPED the tiny beaded handbag the shop girl had assured her went with her outfit. Which wasn't all that difficult considering that the purse looked as though it had been designed for a Barbie doll rather than a grown woman. But it was cute and so unlike anything she would normally buy for herself that she'd decided to go for it. And she now stood staring at where it lay on the sidewalk, wondering how she was going to pick it up.

She started to bend.

"Ah...I wouldn't do that if I were you," Michael rumbled from behind her.

The sidewalk outside Lolita's was hot enough to steam rice on. Kyra could feel the heat shimmer up the parts of her legs not covered by her stockings. It filled her with a sense of anticipation that hardened her nipples. At least, that's what she told herself. That Michael's distracted behavior since she'd emerged from the bathroom might have anything to do with her feelings was too complicated to consider.

Kyra tapped her finger against her glossy lips and considered her dilemma. She'd have to rethink the way she went about everything from here on out. If she had bent to retrieve the bag, as she would have done naturally before, she would redefine the term "mooning" with a view of her hot-pink thong panties. Crouching would have given anyone in front of her a view from the other side.

Michael cursed under his breath and snatched up the bag for her. "What do you have in there? Your lip-stick?"

"Lip gloss," she corrected. And that's about all that fit into the bag. She didn't see the point in carrying it at all, really. Except that it had been nice to watch Michael pick it up for her.

She smiled at him and continued toward the door of the club.

She felt fingers encircle her bare arm and gasped when Michael jerked her back and away from where she was about to open the door.

"You're not going in there," he said for the fifth time since they'd left her apartment.

"Why not?" she asked. Hopefully now that they stood outside the club she'd get an answer. Before he'd merely gaped at her, doing the fish-out-of-water-mouth-moving bit.

"Because you look like...that," he finally said.

"Michael, we've been over this. This—" she gestured at herself "—is the new me. And the sooner people get used to it, the better off for everyone."

"I'm never going to get used to it."

She reached out and patted his cheek. If her hand lingered a little longer than it should have, it was because she enjoyed feeling his stubble sting her skin she told herself. "You will. You'll see."

From behind his back he produced a lightweight jacket she recognized as his. She knew he kept it in the back of his SUV for winter early-morning golf outings.

He tried to drape it across her shoulders and she successfully stepped away from him.

"What are you doing? It's hot as blazes out here."

"But the air-conditioning is on in there."

"Good," she said, "maybe it will cool me down."

"No, you don't understand," he said, his gaze dropping to her neckline. *"The air conditioner is on in there."*

She stared at him blankly. "You're not making any sense, Michael. Now, will you stop being such a stick-in-the-mud and come on?"

She heard him mutter a line of curse words and felt her smile widen. She found she liked frustrating him. He was usually the one in control, the one giving her advice, the one always solid and commanding. That she had managed to gain a little bit of control in their friendship made her feel...well, powerful somehow. More adult. And more than just a little sexy.

At this time of day the club was jumping, filled to the rim with the "after work" crowd that had decided to stay, and the night crowd that was just getting started. Kyra did a once-over, immediately knowing that the person she was looking for wasn't there.

She mentally stumbled, but refused to let that detail stop her. She headed for the long, art-deco bar instead of one of the tables and slid on to one of the stools.

"Hiya cutie." John Boy, the 'tender, greeted her with a grin and a bowl of peanuts. "What'll it be?"

"The usual, J.B.," she said, smiling.

Michael appeared at her side, scowling at the guy who was drinking in his visual fill of her on her other side. "Would you stop," she admonished with a jab of her elbow. "How's a girl supposed to make new friends with you scaring everyone off?"

The 'tender put an unfamiliar drink in a shot glass in front of her. "You want a beer chaser?"

Kyra raised her brows. "What's this?"

"Jim Beam."

J.B. Jim Beam. Kyra felt like giggling. She'd been coming to the club for four years and not only didn't John recognize her, he'd missed his own nickname. Her usual drink was a Virgin Mary, with the emphasis on virgin. She'd never ordered beer much less hard liquor before.

"You're looking a little happy with yourself," Michael muttered under his breath, accepting a brew from John.

"He doesn't recognize me," she whispered, leaning closer to him. She caught a whiff of his cologne. A new scent that subtly coated his skin and made her mouth water with the desire to see if it tasted as good as it smelled.

He turned his scowl on her. "Of course he doesn't recognize you. I bet *you* don't even recognize you."

She crossed her legs, conceding the point. "This is even more fun than I thought it would be."

"That's hard to believe." Michael downed half his beer then dragged the back of his hand across his mouth, looking a little rumpled and agitated, and completely unlike the Michael Romero she knew. "You were enough of a jerk magnet before. Now..."

Kyra picked up the shot glass, trying to figure out how one went about sipping a drink of this nature.

"You're supposed to down it all at once," Michael said, a challenging spark in his dark eyes.

"But wouldn't that get me drunk?"

"That's the point."

She twisted her lips and stared at the drink again.

Her reluctance stemmed from a long-standing dislike of anything having to do with alcohol—any alcohol. She'd grown up with a father who'd drank not to get drunk but to sustain a constant drunkenness. She knew what this presumably innocent-looking poison could do to a person. How it could destroy lives. Distort judgment. Render virtual monsters. It was one of the reasons she'd stayed so far away from anything alcoholic. Except for that one time... The night of her sixteenth birthday. She swallowed hard. She and Alannah had been split up, Alannah to a foster home while she'd been placed with a distant aunt.

She'd hurried home to her aunt's trailer from her part-time job after school, hoping against hope that her aunt had remembered her birthday just this once. She'd found the cake she'd bought and put in the refrigerator the night before on the table, half-demolished, a fork sticking out of the center of the candles. There'd been a half bottle of vodka next to it, the tipped-over contents soaking what remained. And the money she'd saved, wrapped in foil and stored in the freezer, had been gone. She'd come across her aunt passed out over the side of the bathtub, apparently in the midst of taking a shower.

She'd cleaned her aunt up and put her to bed, thrown away the cake, searched for the vodka bottle her aunt kept stashed in her underwear drawer and walked out to the tree swing. There she had alternately swung and drank until she'd puked her guts out.

She'd never touched another drop again.

Unlike her aunt, who to this day still hoped her niece would finance a trip to the liquor store every time Kyra visited the shadowy trailer outside Memphis.

Kyra's gaze trailed to Michael and his intense expression. She hadn't told him that particular story, but he knew many of the details of her background. Her heart swelled at the empathy in his dark eyes while another part of her perked up in challenge.

With more nonchalance than she felt, she said, "Here goes nothing," and downed the fiery amber liquid.

"Here goes everything," Michael said, and motioned to John. "Bring her a beer."

Kyra held her breath, waiting for the burning sensation to pass. Her eyes teared, but she refused to give in to the urge to cough. God, but that was one of the nastiest things she'd ever tasted. Why did people choose to drink such awful stuff?

She gave in and coughed until she was afraid her stomach would end up on the bar in front of her.

Attractive thought.

"Come here often?" she heard a male voice say at her elbow.

A giggle that shocked even Kyra bubbled up from her throat at the terrible come-on line. "All the time."

She glanced at the man in question. She'd seen him in the club a number of times, but had never talked to him. Word had it that he worked at the insurance agency up the way.

"Buzz off, buddy," Michael said.

Kyra elbowed him and turned her attention to the other man. "I'm Kyra White," she said, extending her hand.

The man warily eyed Michael, then took her hand. "Charlie Schwartz's the name, insurance is my game."

"Nice to meet you, Charlie."

His gaze budged slowly from Michael back to her and he leaned forward. "Who's that?"

She jabbed a thumb in Michael's direction. "Who, him? You mean aside from being a major pain the butt?" She smiled at both men, earning a scowl from Michael and a grin from Charlie. "He's my best friend."

Charlie sidled up a little closer to her. "Sounds like a position I might be interested in."

"Give me a break," Michael said.

Kyra reached for the beer the 'tender had put in front of her. "What? Do you think you're the only man capable of being my friend?"

"I'm saying that Charlie isn't as interested in being your friend as he is interested in seeing what you're hiding under that skirt."

"I have what every other woman has."

Michael eyed her dubiously. "Yeah, but it's one he hasn't seen before."

Charlie leaned closer. "Can I get you another drink?"

"Yes."

"No," Michael said. He straightened from where he was leaning against the bar. "Sorry, Charlie, but this girl's taken. Hit the road."

Kyra laughed. Not as a result of Michael's caveman tactics, but because of the phrase he'd used. "Sorry, Charlie." She hadn't heard those words paired up since that commercial. What was it for? Tuna? She couldn't remember.

She sipped her beer, shrugging when Charlie gave her a questioning gaze. "It was nice to meet you, Charlie."

MICHAEL TRIED to cover Kyra with his jacket but was thwarted again by a simple shrug of those smooth, great-smelling shoulders.

"Would you stop?" she said with a deep sigh, though the twinkle in her green eyes told him she was thoroughly enjoying his attentions.

"Not until you either agree to cover up or leave."

She tugged at the hem of that tiny skirt, calling his attention to the legs it barely covered. He cleared his throat and turned his head away, trying like hell to ignore the heat spreading through his groin.

Kyra tugged on his shirtsleeve in playful rebuke. "What is it with you tonight, anyway?"

He scowled at her. "I don't get what you mean."

"First you try to stop me from leaving the apartment, then you continually try to cover me up, and now you're chasing people away from me. You've never done anything like this before."

"Yeah, well, I could say that you've never done anything like this before, either," he said under his breath. "And those people you referred to aren't people. They're dogs."

Her burst of laughter further irritated him. He rubbed the back of his neck and lifted his bottle, only to find he'd emptied it. He raised his brows and lowered the amber glass back to the bar.

"You don't get it, do you? Even after all these years, and all the jerks you've gone out with, you don't have a clue how the male mind works."

Kyra sat up a little straighter, then recrossed her legs. "Well, then, maybe you should educate me."

Educate her. He didn't want to educate her. He wanted to take her home and lock her up in her apartment, alone, until she came to her senses. "Take that guy, for example."

"Uh-huh."

"He wasn't interested in being your friend. He was interested in checking into the nearest motel room with you."

"Why not his place?"

"Because his wife's probably at his place."

He could tell by the widening of her charcoal-rimmed eyes that she hadn't noticed the wedding band the idiot hadn't bothered to take off before approaching Kyra.

"Got you."

She made a face at him. "I just swapped names with the guy, Michael. Not phone numbers."

"Only because I chased him off."

She visually bristled. "And how do you know that doesn't just prove my point—he wasn't interested in me sexually, but was only seeking out a male-female friendship?"

"Because the type of male-female friendships that guy's after include some extracurricular activities."

"Like tennis?"

"If it includes a bed, yes."

"Bed tennis. Sounds interesting."

Michael cleared his throat. "And short-lived."

Kyra crossed her arms under her newly found breasts. Michael's gaze followed the movement, no matter how hard he fought not to look. "I'm getting the distinct impression you don't like my new look, Michael."

He blinked at her. He loved it. He hated it. He ordered another beer. "If I didn't think the sole intent of it was to get back at a certain someone, I wouldn't mind a bit."

He narrowed his eyes, watching as her skin paled.

"How did you know?" she asked quietly.

"Because I know you."

"And you're saying my new look is not me."

"I'm saying that you can be whatever you want to be, Kyra. But don't change for some jerk who hasn't a clue how much you're worth."

A thoughtful shadow entered her eyes. Michael grimaced and looked the other way, glaring at the guy next to him who was also appreciating Kyra's displayed assets.

"And how much am I worth?" she asked, her words a mere whisper in the loud room.

He accepted a fresh beer. "What?"

"Come on. You heard me, Michael. And you know exactly what I'm talking about."

Well, he'd certainly stepped straight into that one, hadn't he?

"Let's just say, more than ten of the jerks you've dated in the past four months combined."

"That much?"

"More," he said before he could consider the wisdom of the admission.

"I see."

Kyra turned her attention back to her own barely touched beer, running her purple-tipped fingernails up and down the bottle, then tugging at the label.

Uh-oh. He hated when she got quiet like this. Mainly because it meant she was formulating a question he would be totally unprepared to answer.

"I'm hungry," he announced, taking a few bills out of his pocket and flicking them on the bar. "Let's say we go get something to eat."

Kyra laid a hand on his arm. "I say we stay and talk about your love life, instead."

Oh, hell. There it was.

"When's the last time you went out with someone, Michael?" she asked.

"What's that got to do with the price of beer?"

She shrugged, jiggling those sweet swells of flesh. "Hey, if my love life is open for discussion, so is yours."

"Or lack thereof," he muttered.

"Exactly my point."

He stared across the bar at the bottles lined up against the mirror. "Kelly Jackson."

"One dinner doesn't count."

"Penelope St. Clair."

She nodded. "Okay. Yes, you did go out with her a few times. About a year ago. Until she, like everyone else you've gone out with, got tired of running second fiddle to your career."

"Yes, well, maybe I haven't found a woman as driven to succeed as I am."

"What about Janet Palmieri? Phyllis said you two had gone out a time or two before I hired on at the firm."

His partner? He grimaced. Trust the rumor-mongering secretary to fill Kyra in on that unworthy piece of gossip. "Two dinners. Not worth mentioning."

"Maybe that's because you're not willing to put the time you put into your career, into your personal life."

"Hey, I put time into our friendship."

She smiled. "Yeah, you do. Curious fact, that."

"How do you mean?"

"Michael, why haven't you and I ever gone out?"

Whoa. Dangerous question.

He told himself to keep it light. Light was good. Hesitating was bad.

He held her gaze without blinking. "Come on, Kyra. We go out all the time. We're out now."

"That's not what I mean." She continued to mutilate the label on her beer bottle. "Why haven't you ever asked me out?"

"What?" He nearly choked on his own tongue.

"You heard me. You. Me. Why haven't we ever dated?"

"We work together. And besides, I'm not your type."

"How do you know?"

He tried to figure out where she was going with this. "Because you've never asked me out."

"Ha-ha."

He tried to cover her up with his jacket again.

"Try that one more time and I'm going to sock you."

Michael froze, immediately recognizing the threat in her eyes. At some point in the conversation, she'd grown serious. And her expression reflected that. Was it when she'd asked why he'd never asked her out on a *date* date? He'd hazard a yes. But that was a question he wasn't up to answering right now. Simply because he was asking himself the same question.

Another applicant for jerkhood sidled up beside Kyra at the bar. Michael's fingers tightened on his jacket as he moved to place it across the back of the stool.

The guy in a too white suit that screamed "northern transplant" tugged on his lapels and grinned suggestively at Kyra. "I've just come to a conclusion about something."

Kyra turned her attention to the guy and smiled. "Oh?"

"I've decided that I want to come back in my next life as that skirt."

Michael clenched his jaw at the obvious come-on. And nearly ground his back teeth to a pulp when he heard Kyra's easy laughter in response.

She launched into an explanation about how she came about wearing the tight, shiny, sorry excuse for a skirt to the stranger, opening the door to conversation even further. Michael's patience thermometer edged up with each second that passed.

"Mind if I touch it?" the latest jerk said. "I've never seen anything quite like it."

"Oh, sure," Kyra said.

Michael snatched the guy's hand away before he

could make contact with the leather. "Think again, moron."

"Michael!" Kyra stared at him in open shock.

"Come on," he said, planting his jacket over her shoulders along with his hands. When she tried to wriggle away, he tightened his fingers until she gave a little yelp of pain. "We're getting out of here."

"Michael...oh!"

He practically hauled her off the barstool, telling himself he didn't care if she broke an ankle when she stumbled in those sexy—ridiculous heels. He didn't stop until they were standing outside the door, much as they had the night before, but this time for entirely different reasons.

"I can't believe you just did that," Kyra said, her face flushed, sparks lighting her remarkable green eyes.

"Yeah, well, believe it," he said, allowing her to shrug out of the jacket now that they were outside in the thick August heat. "It was either that or I was going to hit the guy." He leaned closer to her. "Don't tell me you bought that stupid come-on line."

She thrust out her chin, putting her face even closer to his. "It was original. And he was nice."

"He was a jerk."

"Well right now, you're the only one acting like a—"

Michael wasn't sure how, when or why it had happened. One moment he'd been arguing with her, the next his gaze had fastened on her animated mouth, and he'd been filled with such an urgent need to kiss her that he...well, he did.

And the instant his lips met hers, he knew he was a goner.

Somehow he'd always known, deep down inside, that kissing Kyra would be a life-altering event. She'd bitten most of her shiny lip gloss away, leaving only the smooth, plump texture of her lips. So full. So warm. So inviting. So damn irresistible.

Her eyes were wide and full of disbelief. But Michael couldn't help himself. With a soft groan he thread his fingers through her spiky blond hair and hauled her closer, shuddering when she went boneless against him, her lips parted, her tongue darting out as if in anticipation of his next kiss.

Wow....

Kyra opened up under the assault of Michael's decadent mouth. The equivalent of a Fourth of July fireworks display exploded in her mind, the next burst bigger than the last, until her toes curled up tight in her high-heeled sandals. All she could think was that it was a good thing Michael was holding her up or she would have collapsed to the sidewalk in a puddle of steaming lust.

Oh, sure, she'd often times wondered what it would be like to kiss Michael. But that was usually when she was in bed by herself late at night, reading her latest favorite romance novel. And if she got a little carried away in the shower from time to time with thoughts of Michael's grinning face running through her mind, well that was between her and her handheld shower massager.

But the real thing...wow! The real thing was proving to be better than anything even her favorite romance novelist could have cooked up. As Michael's tongue plundered her all too willing mouth, she thought each and every one of her cells would fuse into the next until she wasn't so much a separate entity but rather a physical part of the man kissing her.

Behind her, the door opened, causing Michael's shadowy dark eyes to open along with it. A spark of recognition seemed to hit him at the same time it hit her and they jumped away from each other as if burned. Which wasn't so far from the truth, Kyra thought as she fought to catch her runaway breath. What she'd felt, while held so close to him, had come very close to the sensation of being burned.

And it wasn't going away.

"I can't believe I just did that," Michael said, pacing a short distance off, then back again. He stared at her as if looking for some sort of explanation on her face, but all she could do was drag the back of her hand sluggishly against her very-well-kissed lips.

"All I've got to say is that whoever taught you how to kiss...well, they did a really, really good job."

Amusement briefly backlit his dark eyes, making them even more attractive. And dangerous. "You're not too shabby, either."

"Jason Monroe. First grade."

"Early starter, weren't you?"

"Oh, yeah. I never leave any stone unturned."

At least she usually didn't. But even as she gawked at Michael, she realized she was staring at one of the biggest stones she'd ever encountered, smack-dab in front of her. And, oh, boy, did she ever want to turn it over.

Confusion warred with need in Kyra's tingling body. Michael had always just been her best friend. He wasn't attracted to her. She wasn't attracted to him. At least that's what they'd always told each other. Even if Michael's mouth had just whispered something altogether different to her. And despite the need rushing through her body, so thick and so all-consuming she felt dizzy.

Lust. Pure and simple. That's what it was between them. After all, how long were two attractive, like-minded people supposed to be around each other without something happening?

Could it be that Michael wanted to see what she was hiding under her skirt, as well?

He ran his hand through his hair and sighed, his expression concerned even while desire shone from the depths of his eyes. "What say we forget that just happened, huh?"

She nodded numbly. Forget that it happened. Sounded like a plan to her. Right now, she didn't have the mental capacity to think beyond that. And she was relieved that Michael had come up with a solution. She was also a tad disappointed. Okay, maybe more than a tad. Maybe a dark, quiet part of her wished he would push her up against the rough stucco wall of the bar and take her right then and there. Give her a full crash course on what else she had missing out on by keeping Michael as her friend instead of her lover.

She shivered, even though it was so hot outside, tendrils of her hair stuck to her damp neck. Michael's gaze dropped to the front of her shirt, no doubt looking at where her nipples were hard and achy, pressing against the front of her tank top like two heat-seeking missiles with him as the target. His gaze was like a caress, fluttering over her barely concealed body and urging her shiver into a full-out shudder that nearly shook her clear off her heels.

Mercy.

He finally turned his head away and loudly cleared his throat as more patrons exited the bar. As the strangers began walking in the opposite direction, the repetitive sound of their shoes on the pavement seemed to mimic the thick cadence of Kyra's beating heart.

"Come on, let's get out of here," Michael said, taking her arm and leading her toward the parking lot.

4

Section II:
Be the part, don't just play it

MICHAEL HADN'T gotten a wink of sleep last night. He'd lain in the twisted sheets, stared at the ceiling and tried to make some sort of sense out of what had happened over the past forty-eight hours.

And now his lack of sleep was showing. It was near noon on a Friday and he'd reworked the same segment on the schematic at least five times, seemingly unable to draw a straight line. He caught the irony. He couldn't seem to move from point A to B in his personal life, either, so why should his professional life be any different?

And that was the problem, wasn't it? Never had he allowed his personal life to interfere with what went on at the firm. His partners occasionally had something or other come up. A weekend extended while on vacation. A missed appointment because a personal lunch had gone long. But not him. Never him. He took care to make sure that what went on at home didn't impact his job performance. It's what helped make the firm what it was today. And it had kept his life simple and uncomplicated.

He brushed off the schematic on the drafting table in front of him then sat back and sighed.

"Holy shit," he heard one of the junior architects exclaim from the table across the narrow hallway next to him.

Michael glanced over to watch the twenty-five-year-old practically reenact a scene from *The Exorcist* as he craned his neck to watch one particularly decadent-looking Kyra step from her office and walk down the hall to the secretary's desk.

The blue pencil in Michael's hand snapped cleanly in two as Kyra bent to say something to Phyllis, her tight purple dress inching up the back of her long, slender legs.

Sometime during the night, he'd comforted himself with the likelihood that Kyra would have cured herself of whatever ridiculous bug had made her dress up as she had and that this morning she would return to the old Kyra he had known and loved and could keep his hands off.

But, no. He'd looked up from his drafting table shortly after clocking in to find two perky breasts even with the edge of his drafting table, the neckline of her dress even shorter than the tank top she'd worn last night. And the three times she'd come out to see to one thing or another, seven male employees had gone into a lust-induced trance, no good to anybody until at least ten minutes after Kyra went back into her office.

Of course, he didn't miss that the three female employees frowned after her much the same way he was doing. Only he suspected for entirely different reasons.

"Ready for lunch?"

Michael blinked, bringing Kyra and her vivid purple dress into focus. Heat sizzled along his nerve endings and for a minute, he was afraid he wouldn't be able to get up.

"Lunch?"

"Yeah," she said, smiling. She had pink lip gloss on today. "It's Friday. We always go out to lunch on Friday."

"Friday."

She laughed. "Earth to Michael." She came to stand next to him. "What's the matter? Having trouble with the Neville account?"

Michael quickly rolled up the plans in front of him to conceal the holes he'd worn in the paper erasing things. "Actually, Kyra, I think you and I need to have a little talk."

"Good. We can do it over lunch."

Somehow a normal lunch with her didn't seem all that normal anymore. Not looking the way she did. And certainly not feeling the way he did.

"I think we should have the talk here." He got up from the chair. "Let's go to the conference room."

"WHAT DO YOU MEAN my new wardrobe isn't appropriate for work?"

Kyra gaped at where Michael leaned against the conference-room table, his arms crossed over his broad chest. His skin looked even darker contrasted against the snowy whiteness of his long-sleeved shirt. He'd rolled up the sleeves, revealing his corded forearms and crisp dark hair.

Try as she might, she'd been unable to do as they'd agreed and forget that last night's kiss had never happened. She'd awakened to the sound of Mr. Tibbs's yowl because at some point, she had squeezed the cat to her chest, obviously a little too hard. Mr. T. had not been happy. Neither had she, for that matter. She seemed to be little more than a walking collection of hormones, her every thought beginning and ending with Michael.

She hadn't banked on *that* when she'd picked up *Sex Kitten 101* and set out to reinvent herself. Yes, she admitted, she had been stung by Craig's crass words about her lack of expertise in bed. And, again yes, she supposed her desire to get back at him had been somewhat at the root of her makeover. But the truth was, whenever she'd looked in the mirror before, she'd barely seen herself. Instead she'd seen details. The fact that her teeth needed brushing, her hair needed trimming, or a zit had broken out on her chin. Now when she looked in the mirror, she saw...well, her. Her appearance said, Wow! Zing! And she felt both of those words to the bone.

Especially when she caught Michael looking at her as though he wanted to eat her whole.

The problem was, he wasn't looking at her that way now. Now...well, he looked pissed.

She crossed her arms under her breasts. "Nobody else seems to have a problem with my clothes. I don't see why you have an issue with them." She shifted on her shoes, already feeling more comfortable in the high heels. "In fact, I've received no fewer than three compliments this morning."

He pointed a finger in her direction. "That's my point exactly."

"What? That people are complimenting me?"

"That people—male people, in particular—are paying attention to you at all."

"Come on, Michael. I've worked here for four years. Everyone here is my friend."

"You might want to try asking some of your female co-workers what they think," he said under his breath.

"Pardon me?"

"Nothing." He pushed away from the table and stepped closer to the door. Kyra craned her neck to see four nearby employees nearly falling off their chairs to see what was going on in the conference room. Michael cursed under his breath and closed the door. A door that was never closed, even during important meetings.

Kyra smiled. "They're going to think something... unprofessional is going on in here."

"Which proves my point even more."

"How so?"

"Before, the thought would never have entered their minds."

"You mean, when I was plain-Jane White?"

"There was nothing plain about you, Kyra," he said quietly. "I happened to like plain Kyra."

"Well, I didn't."

He cocked a brow.

"Well, at least not until after I got to know the new Kyra."

Michael stepped to the sideboard and poured two glasses of water from a metal carafe left over from a morning client meeting. He handed her one then took a deep gulp from the other.

"So is this Michael, my boss, speaking?" she asked. "Or Michael, my friend?"

They had never had to differentiate between the two

before. Now that they were, they stared at each other
curiously.

"The friend. Because if it was Michael, one of the
partners of the firm, I'd be talking to you about the accounting error another partner picked up on while going over the books this morning."

Kyra nearly dropped her glass.

Michael waved. "Forget I said that. Janet's going to
call you into her office to clear everything up this afternoon." He sighed and rubbed his thumb and index fingers against his forehead. "Look, Kyra, I know you
think I'm just being overprotective with the clothes
thing, but I'd appreciate it if you could step back for a
moment and see things from my perspective."

She twisted her lips. "Go ahead."

"Okay. Try seeing all the male employees following
your every move, every time you step out of your office, putting them ten minutes behind in whatever
they're doing."

"They're watching me?" she asked, feeling warm at
the thought. No one had ever watched the old Kyra.

Michael grimaced. "Now multiply that ten minutes
by, what? How many times have you come out of your
office this morning? Three?"

She took a sip of the liquid, surprised he'd noticed.

"That's thirty minutes of lost time."

"I can always stay in my office," she said, teasing
him.

"Then they would all find some reason to pass your
office, or come into it." He put his water glass down on
the conference table. "Kidding aside, do you know
where I'm coming from here?"

"Uh-huh."

"Good."

"But it doesn't mean I'm going to dress any differently."

"Kyra..."

She put her glass down next to his. "Now it's your turn to see things through my eyes. What you're saying is coming awfully close to sexual harassment."

"Bullshit."

"Is it?" She twisted her lips. "Let me ask you this. If Phyllis were to wear the same outfit I have on now, would you be saying anything to her?"

His expression turned pensive.

"No." She cleared her throat. "What you're saying is that a few employees are having a hard time controlling themselves. I don't see how that's my problem. In fact, I think that maybe it's them you should be talking to right now. Not me."

So there, she said mentally.

His eyes darkened. Kyra's throat tightened. She recognized that look. It was the same one he'd worn last night. Right before he'd kissed her.

She squinted at him, doing as he asked earlier and trying to get a look at the situation from his eyes. She was unprepared for the shock of electric attraction. The tingling in her breasts. The sheer desire to kiss him.

She stepped closer to him and he took a step back, putting his rear even with the conference table again.

"You know, Michael," she whispered, placing her palms on his shoulders. "You can be such a rotten stick-in-the-mud...."

Then she kissed him.

HOLY COW.

Michael was so taken aback by Kyra's advances that he could do little more than stare at her as she licked those plump lips of hers, then pressed them wantonly against his.

Even as his lips responded, his tongue dipping out for a much-needed taste of her, he knew that this was crazy. Completely loony-bin-material insane. Not only shouldn't they be doing this, they shouldn't be doing it at work.

"Mmm."

Kyra's hum seemed to vibrate straight through him as he melded his mouth to hers, delving deeper, his hands sliding to her hips and hauling her against him where he leaned against the conference table.

"Michael..."

"Shh," he said, collapsing back on top of the table and pulling her with him until she was straddling him, her dress hiking up to give him a bird's-eye view of her matching purple panties and her swollen womanhood just beneath the silky fabric.

Michael knew he should stop, but before he could act she positioned her arms inside his and pushed them outward, forcing him down to the table. Apparently overcoming her initial hesitation, she followed, pasting her mouth against his again and putting the womanhood he'd just been admiring in very close contact with his immediate arousal.

Even as he threaded his fingers through her spiky blond hair, Michael tried to remind himself of the many reasons why they shouldn't be doing this. But his body wasn't having any of it. It wanted the woman straddled across his hips, and it wasn't going to stop until he had her.

He skimmed his hands down over the soft, stretchy fabric that covered her back then squeezed her curvy rump, pressing her even harder against him.

He groaned, in worse shape than he ever thought possible. Never had he lost track of where he was. But he wasn't about to forget who he was with.

This was Kyra. His best friend. The girl who changed boyfriends almost as often as she changed panty hose.

Only she wasn't wearing any. Panty hose, that is. And she was between boyfriends. And as their conversation last night had driven home, it had been a while since he'd been with a woman.

Aw, hell.

He dragged his fingers against her decadently bare legs then up again, reveling in the softness of her skin.

"Michael?"

"Hmm?"

He heard Kyra's voice try to penetrate the thick cloud of desire, but he was helpless to stop kissing her, to stop touching her. He steered his fingers in the direction of her crotch. He collapsed against the hard table when he felt her slick heat through her silk panties.

"Michael!" This time she pushed away from him.

It took herculean effort to open his eyes. And when he did, he found himself staring at the conference room ceiling.

Work. He was at work.

And he'd nearly just inhaled Kyra.

He glanced at where she straightened her dress, her green eyes wide with disbelief, her skin flushed.

"Wow. I never knew you felt that way about me."

She scrunched her blond spikes. "It's the clothes, isn't it?"

"How I feel about you?" he repeated dumbly, managing to peel himself off the table. "What are you talking about?"

She paced a short distance away and gestured toward him. "I kissed you because, well, I was trying to see things through your eyes."

His brows shot up so fast he was surprised they didn't shoot straight off his face. "My eyes?"

She nodded. "Uh-huh." She frantically paced in front of him. "And right now I don't know what to make of it." She stared at him. "Either I'm the worst kind of voyeur. Or a lesbian."

Michael caught himself grinning.

Kyra pointed at him. "Don't you dare laugh, Michael!"

"Why not? If anything is worthy of a laugh, it's what you just said."

She made a face at him. "Now, tell me what Janet wants to talk to me about. She went over the books earlier this week. Why would she look through them again?"

Michael stared at her and her ability to be so composed after what had happened between them. "What?"

He squinted at her. Despite her abrupt change of subject, he didn't think she was as put back together as she would have him believe. Her skin was flushed. Her breathing still uneven. Yet she forged ahead anyway, confounding him even further since she had been the one to kiss him...no matter the bizarre reason.

"I mean, I know there's an error. I found it yesterday. And I'm having a damnable time trying to figure out where it originates. But I've never been called in for a simple miscalculation before.''

He rubbed his face with his hands, the scratching sound helping him to concentrate.

"Well, there was that one time..."

Michael watched her bite her bottom lip. Undoubtedly she was remembering her first week on the job, when his partners had wanted to let her go because of a whopper of a miscalculation that had taken a week to straighten out.

She looked at him, her green eyes almost knocking him back over the table. "You don't think I should be afraid for my job, do you?"

"Of course not. I'm sure it's not all that serious. Janet just said she wanted to discuss it with you, is all. Nothing to worry about."

She stood staring at him, the quiet time giving him space to rethink the past ten minutes.

Had he really just made out with his best friend?

He dragged the back of his hand across his mouth and came away with pink lip gloss.

Yeah, he definitely had just made out with his best friend. Not only had he just made out with her—if she hadn't called a halt to things, he was afraid he might have tugged her little panties down her legs and done much more than made out with her.

He wasn't sure which bothered him more. That he came so close to doing just that. Or that Kyra was acting as if they had done nothing more serious than discuss the weather.

Kyra turned away from him, then opened the door.

Michael scurried to cover up any proof of his momentary lapse in judgment.

"Where are you going?" he asked.

"To try to fix the problem before Janet asks to see me."

"And lunch?"

She blinked at him as if he'd gone light in the head. "I'll get something from the machine. See you later?"

"Later?"

She smiled. "Yeah. If you're not feeding me now, I think it's only fair that you feed me later."

"Later..."

Michael haplessly watched her saunter from the room on those outrageous heels, telling himself he wasn't going to look. Instead his gaze dropped to her plump rump. He nearly groaned out loud, virtually detecting his handprints on the velvetlike material.

He ran his hands through his hair then walked out of the conference room after her.

"What?" he practically barked at one of the associate architects.

The guy scrambled to get back to work, while Michael sat at his stool, unrolled the plans and stared at the blueprints stretched across the board.

What in the hell was he going to do?

5

LATER THAT EVENING Michael had everything sorted out. He sat at the table at the Mexican restaurant nursing a beer and waiting for Kyra to arrive. While, yes, he'd be the first to admit that there existed a strange kind of chemistry between him and Kyra when they kissed—although she seemed determined to ignore it—becoming involved with her on an intimate level would be the biggest mistake of his life.

Forget that such intimacy would obliterate their friendship. If he took things any further with Kyra—explored just how hot he could coax the sparks that flew between them—he'd be little more than a rebound guy, just a fill-in after her record-setting three-week relationship with Craig Holsom. And that title didn't interest him in the least. Not only would he be flushing their friendship down the toilet, he'd guarantee that their tryst wouldn't last a week. Rebound relationships never lasted long. He'd come to know that firsthand. First there would be the fantastic sex...

His mind wandered to smooth, slick flesh, glossy lips and swirling tongues.

Where was he?

Oh, yes. His disinterest in playing rebound guy to Kyra's desire to get over the latest jerk.

After fantastic sex, they would wake up one day and look at each other and figure out that this isn't what they wanted at all. Kyra would be ready to go back out and conquer the jerk world. And he'd be left helplessly watching after her. Even if they tried to move back to friendship status, it would never work. He'd barely been able to tolerate her boyfriends before. Once they were intimate, and he knew exactly what Jerk Number Fifteen would be gifted with, he'd go insane.

In the corner of the family-owned Mexican restaurant, a mariachi band started up. He grimaced. What was he thinking? Odds were that the sparks that flew between him and Kyra wouldn't see them into a bedroom. He'd been trying to work out the shift in his feelings for her, and figured that the whole uncharted-territory angle was the only reason why either of them was even remotely attracted to each other. Likely they'd reach the point of no return...and run screaming in the other direction. He'd blink and she'd turn back into his best friend, a woman he'd always viewed as a sister.

Well...that he tried to view as a sister, anyway.

"Sorry I'm late."

Michael blinked up to where Kyra was straightening her short, short skirt, then awkwardly trying to sit in the chair across from him without giving the world— and him—a peep show. He caught a glimpse of white cotton panties and figured she'd failed.

"You changed," he virtually croaked, then took a deep swallow of beer to clear the frog from his throat.

"Yeah." She flashed him a smile and dug into the chips and salsa on the table. She shrugged, causing a black lacy strap to bow down over one shoulder. She absently pushed it back up. "I couldn't come out to dinner in my work clothes."

Michael raised his brows. "I thought we'd already discussed that that purple number you had on earlier was not proper work attire."

"And I thought I already told you that what I wear to work doesn't matter, that it's my job performance that counts."

"So long as everyone's clear on what job you're performing."

She crunched down on a chip. "What are you saying?"

He leaned back in his chair, irritated to find that every muscle in his body was as tight as the shirt she had on. "That you could just as easily take up residence on a seedy corner and offer twenty-dollar blow jobs."

She stared at him, openmouthed. "I don't know whether to be insulted or flattered."

"Insulted is what I was going for."

The side of her mouth budged up into a half smile. "I figured that much out." She wiped salt from her hands. "But I figure I'd probably charge at least ten times the rate you quoted."

Michael nearly choked on his beer. His gaze was drawn to her mouth, painted siren-red for the occasion, and the way she ran a fingertip first over and under it to get rid of any salt residue. Then she ran her tongue along her silky lips, making it all too easy to imagine her unzipping his pants and setting her mind to the task they were talking about.

Aw, hell.

She pointed a finger at him, and for a moment Michael thought she knew what he was thinking. Instead she said, "You know, you're an even bigger stick-in-the-mud than I thought."

Stick...mud. Hard...soft and wet.

The waitress came up, putting an end to Kyra's line of conversation and Michael's increasingly miserable state.

If there was one thing that could divert Michael's attention away from Kyra and her decadent mouth, it was her habit of taking fifteen minutes to order a simple meal. She could never just say "I'll have Number Ten" and be done with it. No. She wanted Number Ten, with a bit of Thirteen, and toss in a taste of Number Five. Oh, and could you put this and that on the side?

He sat back and watched her, ceaselessly amazed that the waitress was able to stand patiently and write down everything Kyra ordered instead of hitting her over the head with the order pad and suggesting that she might be happier eating someplace else.

"Are you done?" Michael asked once Kyra finally stopped talking and looked at him.

She blinked, completely clueless as to what he'd been thinking. "Yes."

He clapped his menu closed. "I'll have the Number Ten exactly the way it is."

The waitress smiled at him, took the menus, and walked away.

Kyra crossed her arms on the table and leaned forward, allowing him a perfect view of her rounded breasts just below the lacy neckline of her clingy shirt. He felt the sudden urge to stick his finger into the collar of his own shirt and pull it away from where it suddenly seemed to be choking him.

"Let's get back to the stick-in-the-mud thing," she said.

Michael nearly groaned. "Let's not."

"You know, I've gotten nothing but compliments on my new attire. When I stopped at the store this morning to get yogurt, the checkout guy said I looked very nice."

"Well, that's it then, isn't it? If the checkout guy likes your attire, then it must be all right."

"Smart-ass."

"Shrew."

She laughed at their usual lighthearted exchange. "If the compliments began and ended with the checkout guy then I would agree with you," she said. "But I just used him as an example." She lifted her hand and held up all four fingers and a ring-bearing thumb. His gaze zoomed in on the new piece of jewelry. When did she start wearing a thumb ring? He grimaced. Next thing you knew, she'd be sporting one of those tongue rings.

His mind ventured back to the whole twenty-dollar issue and he slid a little lower in his chair.

Hell, he didn't have to wait for Kyra to steer the conversation toward sex, he was doing a good job of it all by himself.

He tried to focus on what she was saying.

"...no fewer than five date requests."

"What?"

She made a face. "Are you even listening to what I'm saying?"

"Sorry. A way to fix the Johnson design just occurred to me," he said by rote. He used the excuse occasionally, but usually it was whenever she ventured into a long discussion about the human qualities of her cat.

He wasn't an animal person and the excuse always let him off the hook when she discovered he wasn't listening.

"Ah. Didn't we finish with the Johnson job last week?"

Well, it usually worked.

"Did I say Johnson? I meant Neville."

"Uh-huh. Anyway, what I was saying was that today, alone, I received no fewer than five—count 'em, five—date requests."

"Did any of them bring up the subject of money?"

She stared at him blankly for a moment, then realization dawned. "Oh, you're bad. You went back to the prostitution issue, didn't you?" She thoughtfully ate another chip. "You know, if I didn't know you better, I'd think you were well acquainted with working girls. Emphasis on working."

He stiffened. "What does that mean?"

She shrugged, causing her strap to slide down her shoulder again. "Just that you're not the type."

"The type to pay for it?"

"Not necessarily. You're the type that would never get involved with a woman with a questionable past."

"We've gone back to the stick-in-the-mud thing."

"Not by design, but, yes, I guess we have."

Michael was filled with the urge to tell her exactly what he'd like to do with his stick when the waitress brought their orders.

EXACTLY THE WAY she liked things.

Kyra shifted in her seat and considered the plates the waitress laid out in front of her. That's what she loved about this place. They always got her order right. Too often at other restaurants she had to send things back, have something taken off, or tell them they'd forgotten something. But not here.

She smiled and filled a fork with refried beans, taking the rightness of everything that had happened since her transformation as a sign. A sign that she was moving in the right direction. She glanced over to find Michael frowning at his own plate. Well, except for Michael's strange reaction to the changes she'd made.

"I ordered the Number Ten," he told the waitress.

The girl looked irritated as she took his plate and headed back toward the kitchen.

"How could she have gotten that wrong and everything you ordered right?" he rumbled.

Kyra shrugged and pushed one of her plates toward him. "Help yourself."

He crossed his arms. "No thanks. I'll wait for my own."

She pulled the plate back. "Suit yourself."

It wasn't often that Kyra got to see Michael agitated. She realized that she liked seeing him this way. He was always so in control, able to come up with what she was going to say before she said it. And now... Now he appeared not to know what to make of her. And that suited her just fine.

"So tell me, Michael. What is it exactly that you don't like about my new persona?"

He grimaced and opened his mouth.

She waved at him with her fork. "Besides the prostitution thing."

He snapped his mouth shut again.

She rolled her eyes. "Well, if you don't want to answer that question, why don't you try this one on for size. Why, since yesterday, have you kissed me twice?"

NOW *THERE* WAS A QUESTION, although technically, *she'd* kissed *him* the last time.

Michael gave in to the urge to tug at his collar, despite what the gesture might give away. He was beyond caring what Kyra might think of him and his aberrant behavior. They needed to confront this topic dead-on. Because if they didn't, he saw many more uncomfortable meals looming ahead of them. And perhaps even several more kissing incidents.

"Actually, I think it may have something to do with the whole streetwalker concept." He voiced his thought out loud.

She paused, her fork halfway to her mouth. "I don't get you."

"That makes two of us," he muttered to himself before explaining. "No, really. Think about it. We're friends, right? So that means we can discuss things directly, no eggshells involved."

She wriggled in her chair. "Uh-oh. I don't know if I like where this is heading."

Neither did he. But they needed to go there anyway. "Look at it this way. A man, well he…" He trailed off, caught up short by her narrowed gaze. "Would you just let me finish before you go reacting?"

She slowly took her fork out of her mouth. "Did I say anything?"

"You didn't have to."

She made an effort to make her expression bland. He decided that it wasn't working.

"What I'm trying to say is that, as humans, we respond to certain stimuli."

"Like if you're cold, you put something on."

"Or if you put your hand in the fire, you get burned." He drained his water glass. "Actually, I think that's more action and reaction. If you get near the fire, you draw back. Anyway, what I'm trying to say is that..."

"Uh-huh?"

"That with you looking the way you do, all I want to do is...jump your bones."

Kyra's fork clattered to her plate. She had to scramble to keep it from dropping to the floor altogether. "What?"

Michael gave her a smile that wasn't all that innocent. Not innocent at all, actually.

There was definitely something liberating about speaking the truth.

"I—I see."

Michael's correct order finally arrived and he enjoyed half of it before Kyra finally lifted her gaze from her plate and said, "So what you're saying is that if you were to run around in front of me in a pair of shorts and no shirt all day, that I'd want you?"

He tried to envision the scenario. "I suppose. Yes, in essence, that's exactly what I'm saying."

"So you're also saying that you've never felt the...urge to kiss me before."

Rice caught smack-dab in the middle of Michael's throat.

Kyra smiled. "Shot that theory all to hell, didn't I?"

Then she seemed to realize what he'd just revealed

and she paled. "Oh. Oh! You mean you have thought about kissing me before?"

He grimaced. "I've thought about what it might be like to kiss you before. Yes."

"Really?"

He grinned. "Yes, really."

She gestured with her fork. "And that means...what, exactly?"

"It means that I'm a man and no attractive female is exempt from being fantasy material."

"Except your mother."

"She's not a regular female."

"I didn't think I was, either."

"You're not," he said, his gaze slipping to her neckline once again. "Well, at least you weren't until you started...dressing like that."

"So you're saying that my showing a little skin has whipped your hormones into a frenzy."

He nodded, quite happy with that explanation.

She sighed heavily. "That's just so much bullshit, Michael, and you know it."

He stared at her.

"I haven't changed in any way that matters. I'm the same person now that I was forty-eight hours ago. I changed my hair color, a few items of clothing. So what? What does that have to do with anything?"

"It has a lot to do with it. By dressing the way you do, looking the way you do, you've become a walking, talking advertisement for sex. And no man—and I am a man, if you'll remember correctly—can help but respond in some way to that."

A busboy walked by just as Kyra's spine snapped straight, jutting out her breasts. The boy stumbled and the tray he was holding tipped, dumping the contents all over the floor.

Michael gestured toward the kid. "Exhibit number one."

"I didn't cause that," Kyra objected.

"Yes, you did. You breathed, he noticed, and completely lost his train of thought. Worse, he lost control over his bodily functions." He grimaced at his word choice. "That didn't come out right. I meant that he lost his coordination."

"And how do you know the kid doesn't usually break every plate in the place?"

"Because we've seen him at least a half a dozen times in the past six months and he's never dropped a fork."

Kyra looked at the guy as he scrambled to clean up the mess. "Oh."

"Yes. Oh."

She pushed away her own plate and picked up the dessert menu. But while she fingered through the five-page pamphlet, Michael could virtually see the wheels turning in her beautiful head.

"You know, this flies in the face of almost every conversation we've had since we've become friends."

"Now it's me who's not getting you."

She put the menu down. "What do we usually talk about during dinner dates like this?"

"Dates?"

"You know what I mean."

"I don't know. What?"

"About how great our friendship is. About how nice it is to just be able to enjoy each other without the excess baggage a sexual relationship includes." She met his gaze squarely. "About how men and women can be friends without constantly thinking about having sex with each other."

"Yeah, well, that was when you looked like Shirley Temple."

She puffed out a breath. "Shirley Temple?"

He put his napkin on top of his plate. "Okay, maybe Grace Kelly. Or Julia Roberts. But definitely not Angelina Jolie with her hair dyed."

"You think I look like Angelina Jolie?"

"I said you don't look like Grace Kelly anymore."

She flopped back in her chair. "So what you're saying is that since the moment I came out of the bathroom last night, all you've been able to think about is..."

"The same thing every other male is thinking when he looks at you."

"Can you just answer a question without making a huge generalization."

He leaned forward. "Okay, since you stumbled out of that bathroom last night, all I've been able to think about is having sex with you. Hot, heavy, mind-blowing sex."

Her eyes widened. "Wow. I guess that's an answer." She squinted at him. "Really?"

"Really." Whatever satisfaction he'd gotten from his ability to shock her quickly vanished, leaving him staring bald-faced at the truth. "And it's something I don't want to be feeling."

She remained silent for a long moment. Then she blinked at him. "Why not?"

Did she really just ask that? Wasn't it obvious?

Because he didn't want to be Jerk Number Fourteen on her list, that's why not.

And if he felt like anything right that moment, it was definitely a jerk. An honest jerk, but a jerk just the same.

"I'm going to pretend you didn't just ask that," he said.

"Why?"

"Come on, Kyra, you sound like a five-year-old."

"Well you sound like a ten-year-old by avoiding my question."

"Because we're best friends, that's why. And best friends, if they hope to remain best friends, don't sleep with each other."

"Oh. Yeah. You have a point there."

Oh, boy, did he.

He relaxed a little, feeling better for having this conversation. Now that he'd been able to pinpoint the exact reason for his hot reaction to her, he could battle it head-on.

And maybe Kyra might rethink this entire makeover thing.

The waitress came up, her order pad ready as she looked at Kyra.

"Dessert?"

"No," Michael said.

Kyra smiled at him. "Oh, yes...."

6

KYRA'S FAVORITE ROOM in her apartment had always been her bedroom. It was nearly as large as the living room, with a vaulted ceiling and a long, drop-down ceiling fan. And her partiality hadn't changed with her transformation. There was something ultrafeminine about the neon-pink walls, black ironwork bed and lacy white linens. The overstuffed chair in the corner was a combination of both colors and covered in gold tassels and brocade pillows. It was the one room she could enter and immediately forget about the rest of the world.

Switching off the bedside light, she plopped back onto the ten or so pillows cushioning her against the iron headboard and waited for that sweet feeling to claim her.

It didn't come.

Kyra lay impossibly still for a long time, her arms held stiffly at her sides as she stared at the play of the pink and blue neon lights from a sign outside her window, waiting for the feeling to come.

It didn't.

She frowned and switched on the bedside light again, then pushed up onto her elbows. Well, that didn't make any sense. She'd lived there for three years and her bedroom never failed to whisk her away from the world and off to meet the sandman, a guy she envisioned looking very much like Russell Crowe. But for some reason, she felt as though the world had seeped under her door, creating shadowy, unexplored corners.

Three hours had passed since she and Michael had split up outside the Mexican restaurant. Him looking as agitated as she'd ever seen him, while she'd felt as if she'd grown wings. She'd taken the long way home in her convertible, the hot, whipping wind like restless fingers through her short hair.

But now tension coiled in her stomach and she couldn't sleep to save her life.

Sighing, she glanced to the side table where her new book lay. *Sex Kitten 101.* She picked the hardback up, noticing where the paper cover was already growing tattered with use. She settled back against her pillows again and opened the book to where she left off, absently petting Mr. Tibbs who stretched out next to her.

Ten minutes later, she realized she couldn't remember a single word she'd read.

Okay, now they were entering uncharted territory. She'd never, ever had trouble sleeping. Well, at least not when she was an adult. Her childhood was another matter. But not being able to escape between the pages of a good book, a book she'd devoured at every point up until then, well, that called for emergency measures.

She tossed back the coverlet and watched as it landed on Tibbs. "Ben & Jerry's."

Mr. Tibbs instantly perked up and meowed, following Kyra into the kitchen, all for the change in routine. Kyra retrieved a spoon, then the ice cream, smiling as she realized Michael had gotten her favorite. Then again, of course he had.

She dipped the spoon deep inside the heavenly mixture, took a small bowl out of the cupboard, then padded back to her bedroom. After setting Mr. T. up on the night table with the bowl, she slid a spoonful of ice cream into her mouth straight from the carton. She admitted to a measure of guilt that Michael wasn't there to enjoy it with her, seeing as he'd bought it and everything.

Then again, while she relished calling him the Junk Food King, he never indulged in ice cream pig-outs the way that she did. Maybe it was because he didn't like Half Baked, 2-Twisted? She thought that might be the case. But then why didn't he buy his favorite?

Kyra allowed the cold cream to melt on her tongue.

What was Michael's favorite, indeed?

Her mind went blank.

Well, that didn't make any sense. He had to have a favorite.

Cherry Garcia.

No.

Phish Food.

No.

She made a face and spooned in another mouthful without really tasting it. She stared at the empty spoon. She couldn't sleep. Couldn't read. And now she couldn't enjoy her favorite ice cream.

Okay, something was seriously wrong.

She put the carton back into the freezer, then stretched out on the bed again, stomach first, with her book, determined to concentrate this time.

"'Take what you want...'"

She read the sentence three times before it finally registered. She flopped her forehead onto the open pages. And just what, exactly, did she want?

Michael.

She nearly choked.

She did not want Michael. Sure, maybe she immensely enjoyed throwing off his equilibrium, but she didn't *want him* want him. He was her best friend!

That he also had an awesome chest span, beautifully intense dark eyes, a butt to die for, and a decadent mouth that so knew how to kiss...well, she'd known he'd had all of those attributes before, kissing aside. And she had never seriously thought about him as dating material.

Liar.

Okay. Maybe she had. Once or twice.

She rolled over to stare at the ceiling. When they'd first met four years ago, she'd thought him one of the most attractive men she'd ever met. It had been more than just his physical characteristics, as impressive as those were. There was a nameless something about Michael that sizzled. Something more than his mixed Latin heritage provided, although his dark skin and even darker eyes were tantalizingly sexy. She'd once put his appeal down to his aura. While she always suspected her aura was purple, she'd surmised that his wouldn't be a color, but rather a hot eternal burning flame.

Of course, when she'd first met him, he'd been dating the onetime Miss Tampa, Jessica Dobson. The couple had been six months into their relationship and Jessica—who had never made Miss Florida and whose nursing career had hit a wall because she couldn't define bedside manner much less emulate one—was making wedding noises. Noises Kyra had immediately picked up on at that year's office Christmas party, but that Michael either didn't hear or had chosen to ignore.

A month later Miss Tampa had up and eloped with one of Michael's now ex-best friends.

Not that Michael had seemed too upset by Jessica's abandonment. She remembered thinking that he seemed more depressed about having lost his best friend.

A position, incidentally, Kyra found herself being indirectly interviewed for, had nabbed, and had cherished ever since.

No, she didn't golf with Michael the way Paul Allen had. And she couldn't tell a touchdown from a first down in football. And the mere smell of beer made her wrinkle her nose. But that hadn't seemed to matter. They'd clicked immediately, and fell into a comfortable friendship, a relationship that rivaled even her close connection with her sister, Alannah, and that was saying a lot. She and Alannah had gone through a lot in their lives. But now, finally, it appeared Alannah had found her way. She'd married that yummy Brit, Ben Edwards, and was living her own kind of happily-ever-after in Providence with their pet potbellied pig, Elvis.

Michael skittered through Kyra's mind again, reminding her what she'd been thinking about.

She rolled over again and pounded her pillow. By the time Michael had broken up with Jessica, she'd been going out with... Funny, she couldn't seem to remember his name. But he'd been important enough for her to ignore the fact that Michael was free. Well, at least until the nameless boyfriend broke up with her a short time later.

By then, her and Michael's friendship had pretty much cemented itself and she'd never thought of him in an intimate way since.

Well, okay, there was the odd time he'd come to mind, while she was in the shower with her water massager. But as long as the person wasn't related to you, everything was open game, right? It wasn't as though she would ever tell him that one of the best orgasms she'd ever experienced had been with a fantasy image of him, sharing the shower with her, all slick, soapy dark skin and skillful hands, and even more attentive mouth....

She stretched out her legs and wiggled her toes in the soft, worn sheets. Had she known what a damn good kisser he was, that orgasm probably would have been better yet.

Her gaze drifted toward the bathroom door and the shower massager waiting just beyond. She squashed her eyes shut. No. She couldn't. She wouldn't. Michael was her best friend.

Take what you want...

What did she want?

She rolled over and reached for the phone. She didn't know what she wanted. But she figured there was one surefire way to find out....

MICHAEL SHOOK HIS HEAD to clear the sleep from it. The overly bright streetlights seemed to blind him, and the roar of his SUV engine on the quiet streets lent a surreal quality to the situation.

If Kyra was calling in the middle of the night, then

something was wrong. She never called after ten, or before eight in the morning. She was always the thoughtful one, no matter what was happening.

Was it a case of delayed grieving over Craig Holsom? Michael's hands tightened on the steering wheel. Or maybe Craig had contacted her...

Damn it all to hell. One of the reasons Michael was determined to keep their friendship platonic was because Kyra needed rescuing all the time. But if they got involved, who would rescue her from him? He rubbed his chin, finding it thick with stubble. Okay, maybe he'd be the one needing rescuing. But, still...

He knew Kyra had a sister. Alannah, if his memory served correctly. He'd met her once, a year or so ago, when she'd come for a visit. But in the four years since he'd known Kyra, that was the only time he'd seen her.

He wasn't sure how this family thing was supposed to work. He didn't have any siblings of his own, but he would think that the sisters would spend more time together. Not that Kyra ever made any comment about her sister not being here for her. The last time Kyra had seen her sister was when she'd flown to Providence for Alannah's wedding a couple months ago. She'd invited him along, but he'd had to refuse because he'd been tied up in the final stages of an important contract with a wealthy client who could send countless other wealthy clients the company's way.

He squinted at the clock. One-thirty. He groaned and pulled onto Kyra's street. He exhaled when he didn't see emergency vehicles piled up outside her apartment building. He didn't realize that's what he'd been looking for until he didn't see them.

The building sat in the middle of a long line of others

on a well-traveled route, with small, individually owned businesses on either side of it. The whole street was decorated in Caribbean art deco, but at this time of night, it took on a ghostly tint. He parked his SUV, then climbed out, careful not to close his door too hard for fear of waking Kyra's landlady. If there wasn't an emergency vehicle there now, there would be in no time flat if Mrs. K. caught him sneaking into the building so late.

A young guy stepped out of the door to the apartment building counting bills, then stuffing them into a back pocket. Michael frowned, staring at the teen as he walked. His hat identified him as a pizza deliveryman. The car across the street bearing an unappealing plastic pizza on the roof bore out the suspicion.

Mrs. K.? The possibility that the old battle-ax was ordering pizza this late at night wasn't worth considering.

But if it wasn't Mrs. K., then...?

He climbed the steps as quickly and as quietly as possible, a furtive eye on Mrs. Kaminsky's closed door. He reached the second-floor landing and lifted his hand to knock.

"What are you doing up there at this time of night? And what's all this racket? You tell little Miss White that she knows the rules—my rules—for this apartment building! No visitors after midnight!"

The words blasted Michael from where Mrs. Kaminsky issued them from her position in the downstairs hall. Her hair was up in rollers, her skinny collarbone protruding from an old flowered nightgown.

Michael opened his mouth, but realized there really wasn't anything he could say.

Kyra's door opened and he was abruptly pulled inside without a peep; the wooden barrier quickly closing again behind him.

Michael leaned against the wall and swallowed hard. "I swear, one of these days that old woman is going to give me a heart attack."

Kyra laughed quietly. "She's not so bad once you get used to her. I think she has a hearing problem. That's why she yells so loud. She figures that if she can't hear herself, then neither can anyone else."

"We should be so lucky."

Slowly, Michael remembered the reason he'd just been blasted by Mrs. K. and why he was standing in Kyra's apartment in the middle of the night. He sniffed, then his gaze followed his nose to where a pizza box sat, opened, on the counter that separated the kitchen from the living room.

His gaze slowly returned to Kyra. "Okay, what's going on, Kyra? You scared the hell out of me calling in the middle of the night that way."

The remainder of his sentence stuck jaggedly in his throat. Because he immediately sensed the true reason behind her call. No, she wasn't ill. No, she wasn't hesitant to eat alone. As his gaze roamed over her scantily clad body, he realized one thing and one thing only—Kyra intended to seduce him.

Uh-oh.

KYRA STOOD with her hands loosely on her hips, feeling remarkably bold when she supposed she should be feeling a little vulnerable. And that's exactly what the old Kyra would have felt. Then again, the old Kyra wouldn't have been caught dead wearing the short,

short, ice-blue nightie that fit her like a second skin. "Caught dead" being the key words. The old Kyra had always religiously kept her plain-underwear drawer up-to-date, in case she got into an accident or something. She couldn't believe she used to worry about some stranger catching a peek of her white undies. She'd always figured that, *had* she been raised in a traditional household, that's what she would have learned. So that was the behavior she adopted.

But that was the old Kyra. The new Kyra stood in front of Michael proud and tall and knowingly sexy, the silk of her nightie barely hiding the tautness of her breasts, the flatness of her stomach, or the lines of her very naughty thong panties.

"Holy shit," Michael whispered under his breath, his gaze dark in the dim apartment.

Not exactly the reaction she was looking for, but it would do.

Kyra reached out and grabbed him by the shirtfront, pulling him to her.

"K-Kyra? What are you doing?" Michael asked, his throat working.

She smiled at him, angling her head first one way then the other. "Kissing you, of course."

"Of co—"

Kyra had half expected that since she'd gone into the kiss knowingly, no element of surprise involved, that half the thrill she remembered would have been drained out of the experience. Instead she felt something similar to an electrical shock as she pressed her lips against Michael's. She flicked her tongue out to slide it along his bottom lip. He tasted like sleep. Warm and intoxicating and very, very male.

She vaguely registered that he stood as still as the stone she had compared him to, staring at her as if she'd gone insane, his lips unmoving. She smiled, then renewed her seductive attack, slipping her tongue through his lips and flicking it against his. She was determined to see this through to the end.

"Kyra?" Michael croaked. "What are you doing?"

"Kissing you."

"We, um, already established that."

"Yes, but you're not kissing me back." She slanted her head the other way, then caught his earlobe between her teeth and gave a gentle tug. She caught his quick intake of breath, not giving him a chance to regain control as she pressed her silk-clad body up against his, rubbing provocatively.

Then she caught her breath. Oh, Michael might be saying no, no, no with his mouth and his lips, but his body practically screamed yes, yes, yes. It even arched into hers, his arousal thick and long between them.

"Kyra?"

"Shh. I'm conducting an experiment."

He stiffened further. "What kind of experiment?"

She draped her arms loosely over his shoulders and tangled her fingers into his dark, silken hair. "To see if my theory is true."

She slid her hands down and over his back then to his hips, pressing even more suggestively against him.

"You're talking in circles."

She smiled to herself, taking special note of his inability to refuse her. He might not yet be responding, but he wasn't pulling away, either.

Good. But not great. Not yet.

"No, I'm not. Ask me what my theory is."

He licked his lips and she took advantage of the opportunity to catch and suck on his tongue.

"I don't think I want to know," he said once his tongue was once again freed.

"Come on, Michael. Be daring for once in your life. I can tell you've never done anything like this before. Come on. Try it. You'll like it," she teased.

"I doubt that."

"Come on..."

"Okay, Kyra. What's your theory?"

She slid her right hand around his hip and cupped his hard arousal. She felt the breadth and length of him and nearly swallowed her tongue. Her shower massager had nothing on the real McCoy.

"My theory is that the reason behind our sexless friendship is because of lack of opportunity."

"Lack of opportunity." He stared at her. "We're alone together all the time, Kyra."

She tilted her head, watching as his gaze dropped to the deep vee of her nightie. His pupils dilated and he quickly looked back up to her face. "Maybe availability is more the word, then." She popped the top button of his jeans. "You see, ever since we've met, one or the other of us has always been involved in a relationship." She kissed him again. "When I was free, you were unavailable. When you were free, I was busy breaking in Jerk Number Whatever."

Finally her fingers touched hot, silken flesh. She was pleased by Michael's low groan as his hips bucked against her.

"That's it? That's your theory?"

"In a nutshell, yes." She popped the rest of the buttons until she held his rock-solid flesh in her hand. "But that's not all."

"Kyra..." he said, his voice so raspy she nearly didn't hear him. His breathing was coming in quick gasps, even though he had yet to return her kiss.

"I think it's long past time that you and me—we—finally found out what we've been missing."

Michael finally reacted. And oh, boy, was it everything Kyra could have hoped for...

Grasping her bottom, he lifted her up against him, molding her legs around his hips, his mouth searching for and finding hers and kissing her so deeply she was afraid he was going after her very soul.

Kyra clutched him tightly.

"Where's the bedroom?" he practically growled.

She started to point it out, then realized he knew exactly where it was. "Right where it's always been."

Then his legs were moving, carrying them both toward her private sanctuary and the sexy bed inside. Before he'd gotten there, she'd draped a sheer red scarf over the bedside lamp, giving a scarlet cast to the entire room. Not that Michael seemed to notice. Before she could blink, he'd dropped her on the mattress. She bounced a couple times, then gasped when he launched himself across her, nudging open her thighs with his knees. Kyra's back came up off the mattress as he kissed her again, his mouth hot and wet and hungry.

Mercy...

He kissed her hard again then pulled back to look in her eyes, restlessly pushing her hair off her face then holding tight. "Do you have any idea what you're doing?"

She smiled at him, her gaze fastening on his mouth. She licked her lips. "I'm hoping I'm about to engage in the most fantastic sex of my life."

MICHAEL WAS SO HOT for Kyra he was afraid he would spontaneously combust. Standing in front of her in the other room, forcing himself to remain unresponsive, had been one of the most difficult things he'd ever done in his life. Her mouth was decadently tempting, her body soft and warm. And that little nightgown... The silky material slid sensuously against her curvy body everywhere he touched. And he touched her everywhere. Once he'd finally given in to the emotions pounding through him, he couldn't seem to get enough of her. His mouth moved from her lips to her neck to her breasts like a man gone mad. And each place he kissed tasted better than the last.

He cupped her right breast in his hand through the silken material and she arched up into his touch. She was so beautifully responsive. He'd known she would be. What he hadn't considered was his own response to her responsiveness. Knowing she wanted him did all sorts of funny things to his stomach. And he was so hard he hurt.

Kyra seemed to be having the same problem he was, her hands tugging at his hair, then molding to his rear end, then swerving inward to stroke him with feather-light touches.

Michael threw back his head and groaned. Forget light. He wanted her hard. Hard and fast and all night long.

He caught her fingers, then curled them around his arousal, squeezing tight. She gasped, her eyes on his. Then that little pink tongue of hers dipped out to moisten her lips and Michael thought he might lose it right then and there.

Too much...way too much, way too soon.

But damned if he could stop himself. Once events were set into motion, he knew they wouldn't be able to stop until they reached the end. And that was a point he wanted to keep far off into the distance. If this was to be his only time with Kyra, a tryst that might end their friendship, he fully intended to get the most out of it, damn it.

He removed his hand from hers to sweep the back of his fingers up her flat stomach to the top of her nightie. With a dip of a finger, a perky little breast crested over the top of the light blue silk, a cherry-red nipple just begging for his attention. And he was all too happy to give it what it wanted. He swirled his tongue around and around, drawing tighter circles until he closed his mouth over the engorged bit of flesh. He never knew a woman could taste so good. She was like Sunday pot roast, hot fudge, and a refreshing cold brew—all his favorite things—rolled into one.

She cried out, pressing her breast farther against his mouth. "Please," she whispered. "Oh, please, please, please."

Michael released his grip on her nipple, then ran the length of his tongue over the swollen crest. He remembered her naughty game earlier, asking him questions that he'd been loathe to respond to. And his own desire spiraling higher and higher with each word she uttered.

Two could play at that game.

His fingers found the damp scrap of material between her legs. He tunneled inside the elastic and traced a fingertip over her tight bud then down between her slick flesh. "Please what, Kyra?"

Her eyelids cracked open, revealing green eyes almost black with desire. "What?"

He grinned at her then tickled her wet portal. "What is it that you want?"

He slid his finger up into her dripping wetness. She instantly contracted around him, urging him farther inside as she unconsciously ground her hips against him.

Michael lowered his mouth to her neck, kissing her, then blowing on the dampness covering her skin. "Tell me."

"You," she whispered harshly, her fingernails digging into his back. "I want you. Us. To be joined." She restlessly licked her lips. "Now."

He pulled his finger out then entered her with two fingers, readying her for a more meaningful meeting. "You want to have sex with me?"

She nearly came completely off the bed. "Yes!" she cried. "I want to have sex!"

He removed his fingers then caught her chin in his hand. "With me," he prompted, holding her still.

Her eyes were glazed but cognizant as he gazed at her and she seemed to be having a hard time swallowing. But none of that equaled the hammering of his heart in his chest.

He didn't want this to be sex behind closed eyes. He

wanted Kyra to know who she was making love to. Wanted her to recognize that it was him who moved inside her, coaxing her to climax. And he needed to know that she needed him in the same way.

She nodded her head as best she could in his grasp. "Yes. I want to have sex with you."

That was all Michael needed. He quickly shed his jeans, shirt, put on a condom, then stripped her of her tiny panties. She moved to take off the nightgown, but he held her still. "No. Leave it on."

There was a question in her eyes. But not for long. He entered her in one long stroke, driving straight home, her flesh wet and tight and oh, so very sweet. Her low moan wrapped around him as tightly as her muscles, as he balanced himself on his hands and grit his teeth to keep from climaxing right then and there.

Oh, but she felt so good. So damn right. He looked down to where her nightie covered their joined bodies then peeled the silken material back to reveal just how good they looked together. Kyra restlessly gyrated against him, apparently deciding that lying there waiting for him to continue wasn't enough. His hips bucked involuntarily. He'd never been so close to climaxing so quickly, not even in his teens. He held tight, counting backward from ten.

Kyra bumped her hands against the inside of his elbows, throwing off his balance, then pushed him over to lie flat on his back. Michael wasn't entirely clear on what had happened until he glanced up to find her straddling him, her hair spikier than usual as she tugged off the nightie, allowing him to gaze at her delectable body in its entirety for the first time.

She slowly took him back inside her. Michael reveled in watching her shiver as she adjusted to his size, her stomach muscles taut and well-defined, her breasts pert with nipples seeming almost too large for the smaller mounds. He fanned his fingers around her waist, budged them upward, cupping her breasts, teasing her nipples, then following up along the delicate line of her collarbone and neck. She leaned her cheek into his touch, then kissed his hand, running her tongue along his palm then sucking on his index finger. The feel of her mouth on his hand, and his arousal buried deep in her body proved one of the most excruciatingly erotic moments of his life.

Until she moved...

A groan began somewhere in the vicinity of Michael's groin then slid from his throat like a wolf's howl. Kyra shimmied her hips, moving forward, then back, almost as if in a semisitting position, then sat back again, her bottom hot against his thighs, her heat dripping to cover his skin. He plucked at her engorged nipples. She moaned and reached out to balance herself against the headboard, her fingers curling around the ironwork and holding her upright even as she worked her magic on his body.

Kyra threw her head back and whispered his name as her movements became more frantic, more urgent. Flames exploded inside Michael as he dropped his hands to her hips and watched her through half-lidded eyes. Her breathing came in ragged gasps, her small breasts bounced up and down, her swollen flesh covered him then withdrew only to cover him again.

"Michael!" Kyra called, her back arching, her body stiffening. Michael bucked up against her once, twice, then Kyra melted around him like a shimmering puddle, carrying him along with her.

Kyra collapsed against him, her muscles contracting and convulsing around him. Michael held her tight, held her still, riding out the glorious waves of his own orgasm.

A loud pounding sounded. Michael groaned, thinking it the sound of his heart.

"What are you two doing up there?" a high-pitched voice filtered through the floor, muffled but all too familiar, followed by another bout of pounding. "You know I don't go in for any of that premarital monkey business. I won't stand for it!"

Kyra's body vibrated against Michael's as he lay staring wide-eyed at the ceiling, feeling as though his mother had just caught him with Miss November in the bathroom. He realized Kyra was laughing. He grinned and ran his stubble-covered chin against her cheek. "You think that's funny, huh?"

She pulled back to kiss him. Then kissed him again, her mouth hot and wet. "Don't you? You have to admit, it's not every day a nosy old woman yells at you to stop having wild sex."

God, but she was even more beautiful to him now than she had been before. And doubly enticing. "I noticed she waited until we were done to make her presence known. Does she always do that?"

Kyra lay her head against his shoulder. "I don't know. This is the first time I've invited anyone over."

Michael lay there for a long moment, taking in her words.

"Mrs. Kaminsky has her rules, you know," Kyra whispered.

It seemed Kyra had a few rules of her own, he was just coming to realize. And as he kissed her bare shoulder, Michael felt an intense hunger to get to know every last one of them.

KYRA'S MUSCLES ACHED. She stretched and smiled, recalling the cause for the throbbing, and the man who had given her the best sexual workout of her life.

Michael.

She popped one eye open, then immediately closed it against the morning light streaming in through her window. Too bright. She rolled over and swept her hand across the other side of the bed. Her fingers halted when they met with a foreign object. Either Michael had a hair-growth problem or she was touching Mr. Tibbs. She squinted at the feline lying on the other pillow as if he belonged there and frowned.

"Michael?" she called, rising to her elbows.

No answer. The door to the living room was open, showing the bathroom open and empty, as appeared to be the case with the rest of the apartment.

She quirked a brow. Okay...

She glanced at the clock to find it after ten. A fact that panicked her until she realized it was Saturday and she didn't have to be anywhere that morning. She flopped back onto her own pillow and draped an arm across her eyes.

The first thought to come to mind was...wow. Never in a million years would she have guessed that her best friend was a virtual sex god. Oh, he had the looks that would let him into any girl's panties. But she'd found out the hard way that too many attractive men figured they could get the job done with their looks alone. Either that, or they had been catered to so much of their lives that they didn't have to work hard at anything, including sex.

Not Michael. Michael...

Wow.

Her hand wandered to the other side of the bed again, finding the sheets cold. The panic she'd felt at seeing the time began to creep in around her again. She squashed her eyes shut, fending the acidy feeling off. She would not panic. She would not take Michael's morning disappearing act as a sign that last night hadn't been good for him. She would not even imagine that he regretted what had happened between them. She ran her fingers through her tousled hair, then smiled at the short spikes where once her heavy brown tresses had been. No, she wouldn't think like that. Because that's exactly the way the old Kyra would think. And she wasn't the old Kyra anymore. Oh, no. This was the new Kyra, who didn't overanalyze the men she dated or allow their actions to dictate how she conducted her life. She and Michael had experienced great sex. That was it.

Maybe he'd had to be on the job site this morning.

Kyra swallowed hard. Okay, so maybe she couldn't banish the old Kyra with one wave of her hand. Perhaps she'd have to do this in stages. And considering what had happened last night, she figured she'd leaped over at least a few of those stages in only a couple of hours.

Mr. Tibbs got up from his spot and butted his head against her hand. Kyra absently patted him, then reached for the cordless phone on the nightstand.

"What?" she asked the disapproving cat. "I just want to wish him a good morning."

Mr. Tibbs twitched his tail then leaped off the other side of the bed as if unable to stand watching his mistress make a fool of herself.

"Hey, it's not like I'm going to ask him where he is. Or why he left without saying goodbye or anything. It's Saturday and I want to see what he's up to this weekend. Best friends do that."

Oh, yeah? Then why did it feel like bees were stinging the inside of her stomach?

She pressed autodial then sank back into the pillows again, breathing deeply.

"Hello?"

Michael.

Kyra opened her mouth to speak, then quickly pressed the disconnect button.

A small, strangled sound escaped from her throat as she stared in horror at the receiver. Ohmigod. She did not just do that. She absolutely, positively could not have just hung up on Michael.

Oh, but she had. Which knocked her back at least a decade in the age-old dating game.

She hit herself repeatedly in the head with the cordless receiver. "Stupid, stupid, stupid."

Especially in this day and age, of Caller ID. Not that what she did would have been okay back when you could get away with hanging up on someone without them knowing. But at least it would have been easier to write off the incident as a mistake.

The receiver in her hand vibrated, then let out a piercing ring. She yelped and dropped it, then scrambled to pick it back up. She knew who it was. And she knew that he knew what she had just done.

"Hi, Michael," she said as casually as possible. Which, without any major caffeine, wasn't very casual at all.

"Did you just hang up on me?"

She made a face. "Yeah. Sorry about that. I was..."

She was what? There really wasn't anywhere to go with that. The next best thing would be to redirect the conversation. "Where are you?"

Okay, why didn't she just smother herself to death with her pillow right here and now? God, could she get any clingier? More needy? She groaned, not liking the view she was getting of the old Kyra, the new Kyra... oh, just plain Kyra, period.

Michael's chuckle crackled over the line. "Are you all right?"

"Fine." Except for the pillow she had over her head.

"Sorry I left without saying goodbye. Did you get my note?"

"Note?" He'd left a note? Where?

"I left it taped to the coffeemaker. You know, thinking you'd head there first." She heard background street noises. "I figured it would be a good idea to get out of there before Mrs. Kaminsky got up. You know, to save you from any more trouble."

Mrs. Kaminsky.

Kyra's face burned hot. She'd forgotten about her nosy landlady.

"What are you doing for lunch?" he asked.

Kyra slowly dragged the pillow from her face. "What?"

"Lunch. You know, that meal at the middle of the day? What are you doing for it?"

Jumping off the Howard Frankland Bridge.

"What?"

Kyra bolted upright. Had she said the words?

"I'm at the Neville site now, but I should be finishing up around noon. You want to meet me at, say, one o'clock at Niko's?"

"No." Kyra wondered what was with her mouth this morning. "I mean, yes. Greek sounds good." Actually, the thought of food made her sick to her stomach just then, but what would Michael think if she turned him down?

"Kyra?" he asked quietly. "Are you sure you're all right?"

She gripped the receiver tightly. "Sure. I'm fine."

"You're not, um, having second thoughts about what happened last night, are you?"

She swallowed hard. "No. Are you?"

"No."

"Good."

"Good."

"So, um, I guess I'll see you at one, then."

"One."

The dial tone sounded in Kyra's ear. She slowly pulled the phone back to stare at it, then hit the disconnect button, only to hit it again to get an outside line. The problem was, she was about to call Michael. Not Michael, the guy she had just spent an incredible night with, but Michael, her best friend. You know, to get advice on Michael, her lover.

She put the phone back in its cradle then flopped back, kicking her feet in a mixture of frustration and excitement. What was she going to do? How could she possibly face him for lunch now that he knew about the funny little noises she'd made last night?

She crawled out of bed, retrieved Michael's note from where it was, indeed, taped to the coffeemaker, then padded to the bathroom, deciding to take things one step at a time. First she'd have a shower. Then she'd do her hair, get dressed, and drive to the restaurant. And between now and then, hopefully she would have figured out what in the hell she was going to do about the mess she was afraid she was making out of her life.

She pulled back the shower curtain and came face-to-face with the shower massager. It took some work, but she managed to twist the sucker off the end of the hose and throw it in the garbage can. The damn thing had already gotten her into enough trouble.

MICHAEL HAD THOUGHT he'd known everything there was to know about Kyra White. You weren't friends with someone for four years without learning something. But as he sat across the restaurant table from her he wondered if he really knew her at all.

Oh, she still looked like the same Kyra. Well, at least the one with the spiky bleached-blond hair. She still ordered her meal as if the chef didn't have a clue what he was doing. She still rolled her straw paper into a tiny ball then smoothed it out again only to tear it into tiny little shreds.

"Friends," he repeated dumbly, trying like hell to refocus on their conversation.

He'd arrived at the restaurant at one on the dot and reserved their favorite table. Then he'd waited...and waited…and waited. Finally, somewhere just after one-thirty, Kyra had stumbled into the place, looking uncertain on her high heels, and barely daring to meet his gaze.

Then she'd asked if they could go back to being just friends.

Right…

"I was afraid this was going to happen," he said, leaning back so the waitress could give him his plate.

"Afraid what was going to happen?"

He waited until the waitress left, then leaned forward. "What's happening now. Why do you think I resisted letting anything happen at all, Kyra?"

"Because you didn't want me?" She grimaced and rolled her eyes. "Forget I just said that, please. God, could I be any more pitiful?"

He stared at her as if she'd gone insane. "Are you serious? Is that what you thought?" Okay, he didn't know the woman across from him at all. He never would have guessed that she was the insecure type, given to hanging up on people and needing constant reassurances after what had been, resoundingly, the best damn sex of his life.

He rubbed the back of his neck and picked up his fork, though the prospect of eating didn't really appeal to him.

Truth be told, he hadn't been in such great shape himself that morning. When he'd woken up at six and realized where he was, what he had done and who he had done it with, he'd grabbed some paper, scribbled out a quick note, then run out of the door so fast he'd been out of breath when he reached his car. It had been a long time since he'd spent the night at a woman's place. And after staying over at Kyra's, who was not just any other woman...well, he'd needed a little space to try to sort things out.

Not that that space had helped any. He'd been an emotional mess. He alternately kicked himself for leaving her apartment without saying goodbye, then caught himself grinning like an idiot when he remembered the sex. And through it all, he'd wandered around like a man with no direction, wondering what this shift in their relationship would mean.

Of course none of that mattered now that Kyra had suggested they go back to being friends.

"Friends," he said again, trying to remember the way things had been between them before last night. Before she'd called him, then seduced him, in her sexy little nightie. Before she ground against him, seeking her own orgasm and in the process, giving him one he'd never forget.

Before he'd found out that the woman across the table from him was as wonderful in bed as she was out of it.

"Friends," she said, then nodded.

"Okay." He bit into his gyro then wiped his mouth with a paper napkin. "We can do that."

She finally looked at him instead of staring at her plate. "We can?"

Michael sighed. "Sure. Don't you think we can?"

"I wouldn't have suggested it if I didn't think we could."

"Good."

"Fine."

"Great."

Then Michael met her gaze and knew that they'd end up in bed at the first opportunity...

8

FOUR DAYS LATER, Michael sat at his drafting table at Fisher, Palmieri, Romero and Tanner, unable to concentrate on the work in front of him. He rubbed his closed eyelids, then looked at his watch. It was after 7:00 p.m. Sure, it was late, but he couldn't remember ever feeling this tired. Of course, the late nights he'd been spending with Kyra weren't helping matters. The great sex he'd thought they'd only have the once? Well, they were having it every day, several times a day, anyplace they could find where they wouldn't get caught. And no matter how many times he had her, he wanted her twice as badly again right afterward.

Neither of them mentioned the "friends" conversation again. Which was a good thing, because despite the roller coaster of emotions he found himself on when they weren't together, he was having a damn good time when they were together. Kyra was as inventive between the sheets as she was with her appearance, surprising him in ways no woman had ever accomplished. Coy and demure one time, a wildcat the next, he never knew what he was going to get the instant they were alone together.

What would happen once that flame of passion died out was a question he was putting off answering for when it actually happened. And it would. He knew it would. While their friendship was based on common interests, trust and loyalty, the sex between them... well, it was based solely on pure human need.

In fact, he was starting to think their relationship was a bit like a wicked version of Jekyll and Hyde. He and Kyra would lunch together, go book shopping together, all the time talking and teasing the way they always did. Then the door would close on her apartment and they'd be all over each other, Mrs. Kaminsky and her banging demands be damned.

The role-playing was beginning to take its toll on his psyche as well as his physical demeanor. He didn't know how much longer they could keep this up before something snapped.

He reached for his cold cup of coffee and took a good mouthful, trying to infuse his drained muscles with some much-needed energy. He gave up and dumped the cup and its contents into the trash bin next to his drafting table, then repositioned his work light so that it illuminated a different part of the schematic.

The place had been deserted for the past two hours, since today everyone had clocked out right at five. It was a company-wide hump day ritual that helped the week go by faster. But Michael had stayed behind to get caught up. Tom Neville, his latest and most bothersome client, had changed around the kitchen cabinets—again—and it was up to him to make the new design work. And he wasn't having fun with it. He'd stopped having fun somewhere around the fifth redesign when the construction subcontractor, despite the money the client was throwing at them, started showing signs that he and his men were getting tired of moving around the same countertops and cabinets.

Of course, his conversation with the sole female

partner in the firm, Janet Palmieri, hadn't helped matters, either. All the senior and junior partners had gathered in the conference room for their weekly meeting and afterward, Janet had asked him to stay behind so she might have a word with him. He'd figured she'd wanted his advice on a job, or to enquire further on the Neville account. Instead she had brought up the accounting error that Kyra had, so far, been unable to figure out.

He'd been puzzled as to why she would zoom in on him to discuss the issue, and not take normal channels.

Perplexing him even further was that, midway through the conversation, Janet had waved her hand and told him not to worry about it, that she was sure the problem would work itself out. Kyra would find the error and everything would go back to normal.

"You know what they say about all work and no play, don't you?" A sexy, familiar voice broke the still silence.

Michael blinked to where Kyra stood on the other side of the drafting table wearing the same clothes she'd had on earlier. He grinned at her, feeling the tension seep from his muscles at the mere sight of her, only to be replaced by a whole different kind of tension.

"I didn't know you were still here."

She smiled, her gaze taking in the empty firm. "I could say the same of you."

Michael wondered if the reason she'd stayed had anything to do with the accounting error Janet had talked to him about. But he didn't want to ask Kyra about it. Not just now. Not when she was pulling her shirt over her head, her smile decidedly devilish. He heard the rasp of a zipper, then she was shimmying out of her leather skirt, leaving her standing there wearing only her bra, panties and those naughty high-heeled shoes he'd taken such a liking to lately.

She cleared her throat. "I've often fantasized about what it would be like to be stretched across your drafting table, having you work your magic on me instead of those blueprints."

Without a second thought Michael swept the schematics in question off the table and onto the floor, then hauled her to stand in front of him, the adrenaline flooding his system dizzying in its intensity.

Hell, he hadn't needed caffeine to get his blood pumping. All he needed was one look at Kyra, with or without clothes, to feel refreshed and energized. He skimmed his thumbs over the delicate ridge of her collarbone then down between her breasts and over her arms. With a slight boost, he lifted her onto the table.

She gasped, her sexy laughter filling the otherwise empty room. "Are you sure it will hold me?"

"I'll make sure it does," he murmured, scooting his stool closer, then kissing her stomach.

Damn, but she looked good draped across the top of his table. He didn't think he'd ever be able to look at it again without envisioning her there, all creamy flesh, hard nipples and moist mouth. He pulled his light closer to provide heat in case she got cold and to illuminate his path to his ultimate destination between her long, long legs.

His gaze dropped to the black-and-red panties she had on today and he groaned. He didn't know where she got the never-ending stream of panties, but he wanted to buy stock in the company. The silky fabric was just wide enough to cover her crevice, but narrow enough to let him see her swollen flesh. He skimmed a finger over the damp crotch, reveling in her quick intake of breath.

Running his hands over her legs, he bent them both until her spiked heels rested on the edge of the table. He looked up into her flushed face, drinking in the dark passion in her green eyes.

In that moment, he thought he could live to a hundred and still not have had his fill of the woman who had turned his world on its ear with one simple little kiss. He wanted to taste her, suckle her, touch her, buck into her until nothing else mattered. Until the many problems plaguing their relationship disappeared and left them a mass of satisfied hormones.

He gazed down on her and grinned. "You have another pair of these, don't you?"

"What, underwear? Yes."

"Good." He hooked a finger under one of the lacy sides and yanked, tearing the material instantly. He caught the silk before it could completely fall off, then used it as a barrier as he rubbed it over the tight bud at the juncture of her thighs.

She nearly came up off the table. He held her steady with one hand on her stomach as he swirled the silk around and around, then maneuvered it through her slick folds and back again. Her eyes had fluttered closed. Michael groaned at the complete rapture on her beautiful face, then lowered his head to press his mouth to the delicate places he'd massaged.

Kyra moaned, her hips bucking automatically against him. He laved the button of her arousal, then fastened his lips around it, taking the bit of flesh into his mouth and gently sucking. Instantly she dissolved into a molten puddle of shudders, her fingers wildly tugging at his hair, her hips rocking in motion with his sucking.

"Too quick," he murmured, thrusting two of his fingers into her slick opening before she could respond and drawing her climax out even further.

Several minutes later she lay across the table trying to catch her breath, her skin covered in a light sheen of sweat, shining under the warm yellow light from the lamp.

Her eyes smiled at him when she opened them. "You are very, very bad."

He plucked her flesh. "Oh, you have no idea."

He tugged her hips until her bottom rested on the edge of the table, then unzipped his pants, freeing his throbbing erection. After rolling on a condom he retrieved from his pants pocket, he fitted the knob of his arousal against her wetness. She tried to stretch her legs out to dangle over the side, but he refused her the freedom. Before she could object, he thrust so deeply inside her he immediately got lost in the swirl of ecstasy and pure emotion that went along with having sex with Kyra. His blood roared through his veins, his skin felt on fire, his very skin felt as if it might burn on contact. She grasped the edge of the table and he thrust again, her low moan reaching his ears and causing him to groan in response.

He thrust in, pulled out, each move deliberately slow, designed to prolong their trip, intensify their crisis. And if the time allowed him to revel in her response as he filled her, well, that was a fringe benefit. He parted her thighs as far as was comfortable, then reached up and popped the front opening to her bra, freeing her small breasts.

"So beautiful," he murmured, cupping her sweet flesh.

Kyra threw her head back and clutched at his arms. "Please," she whispered throatily.

He slid all the way home and immediately pulled back again. "Please what, Kyra?"

She blinked at him, knowing she saw the merciless teasing in his own eyes. "Please...harder. Faster." He thrust into her. "Yes. Like that. More."

And more was exactly what he gave her. He rocked in, then out, each thrust faster than the one before. He grasped her hips to hold her steady, ramming into her, giving it to her just the way she wanted it. He watched as her small breasts swayed, her teeth bit her lip, until finally she stretched out her neck and let loose a low cry.

"Oh, yes, yes, yes." She clutched his hands where they gripped her hips. "Oh, yes, Michael, yes."

What could a guy do but follow right after her? He melded then retreated, melded then retreated, until both of them rested on his drafting table, a quivering mass of spent energy.

Michael released her legs, hoping the table wouldn't give way and topple them both to the floor. His legs felt like rubber. His heart hammered so hard he feared it might beat straight through the wall of his chest. He pressed his lips against Kyra's neck then lapped at the salty residue there.

For a long time, he didn't say anything. Merely enjoyed the moment for what it was. And tried not to wish they were lying in her bed at her apartment so that he might drift off to sleep.

Kyra moved first. Actually it wasn't so much a moving as it was a stirring. She subtly rotated her hips, testing the strength of the erection that still filled her.

Michael pulled back slightly, then smoothed her hair away from her face with both his hands. He kissed her. "More?"

Her sexy smile almost toppled him right over the edge again. "Oh, yes. Much more...."

KYRA STUMBLED out of bed the following morning, finding walking close to impossible, her flesh was so raw and swollen. She smiled. At the rate she and Michael were going, they would have made up for the past four sexless years in no time at all. She pushed open the bathroom door only to find the light already on.

"Ooops. Sorry," she said, grabbing for the door handle.

"No problem."

She blinked to find Michael straightening from outside the shower, not seeing to any personal business. "What are you doing?"

He shrugged, looking especially handsome standing there wearing nothing but a grin. "I found the shower massager in your garbage. I was just fixing it."

Kyra stared at the hose, noticing that he had, indeed, fixed it.

She covered her mouth with her hand and giggled.

"What?" Michael asked, scratching his chin.

She shook her head. "Um, nothing. But do you mind? I have some personal business to attend to."

He crossed his arms, his gaze taking in her own nakedness.

"Haven't you had enough yet?" She grasped his shoulders then maneuvered him out the door, soundly closing it after him. His chuckle filtered through the thick wood. "Oh, and make yourself useful. Why don't you make some coffee while you're out there?" she called.

She lowered herself to the commode and eyed the shower massager. If he only knew why she'd taken it off to begin with. She smiled then looked around the tiny bathroom. A day or so ago, he'd brought a toothbrush along with him. She decided she liked seeing it there in the cup next to hers. She also liked the shaving cream and razor in her cabinet, his deodorant and cologne on the back of her toilet seat, and didn't even mind the discarded pair of Skivvies lying on the floor. She stretched out her foot and dragged the underwear toward her, then picked them up. She wondered how Michael would feel about finding her underpants on his bathroom floor.

Then she wondered what the chances were of her actually leaving them there....

Kyra dropped his underwear in the hamper, then finished her business and moved to the sink. The smile she'd been wearing a few moments before was gone, replaced with concern. She didn't like thinking what she was thinking, but she couldn't *not* not think about it, either.

Okay, so last night's escapades on Michael's drafting table aside, they had decided to keep their affair a secret from co-workers and friends. What was happening between them was so...intimate, so very private, it didn't fit within the parameters of other relationships. She couldn't exactly sidle up to the company water-cooler and confide to Phyllis, "Let me tell you, you have no idea what Michael's hiding in those pants." Or call her sister and say, "You remember Michael? Oh, boy, you wouldn't believe how good he is in bed." Or even tell her nosy landlady, "Hey, sorry about the noise. We just can't help ourselves."

No, what was happening between her and Michael wasn't sharing material. At least not yet. Whether it ever would be was a question that still loomed out of her reach. Honestly, she wasn't ready to try to answer it yet. But then she realized that not once over the past week, had she and Michael gone to his place...

What? She rubbed her toothbrush almost violently against the mouth of the nearly empty tube of paste. What did that mean? Maybe he'd fired the maid and the place was a mess. Maybe it had never occurred to him to invite her over.

Or, simply, he might just prefer her place over his.

Yeah, right. She attacked her teeth with a vengeance. Michael had hated her place ever since she moved in. Aside from it being old—he said the word as if it had four letters instead of three—he thought it was on the wrong side of town, and came with a landlady that scared the bejesus out of him.

Before—well, before they'd discovered exactly what they'd been missing out on between the sheets—he'd invited her over to his place all the time. Still, she had to admit, that mostly they ended up at her place. But that was because all the fun stuff to do was located in her part of town. Michael's subdivision was so new, there were few interesting restaurants and shopping centers in the area.

Still....

She squinted her eyes then leaned forward to consider a red splotch on her chin that looked suspiciously like a zit. Great. That's just what she needed now.

Michael knocked on the door. "You planning on coming out of there anytime soon? We're going to be late."

Late? Her eyes widened. Work! Oh, God. She'd nearly forgotten today was Thursday, which meant they both had to be in by nine.

She quickly rinsed her mouth then opened the door, tossing Michael a clean towel. "Leave me some hot water."

He caught her wrist, sending tingles of awareness skittering over her skin. "We could always take a shower together."

Michael and the shower massager all wrapped up in one neat little package? Kyra didn't think she was quite up for that one yet. She smiled and kissed him. "I'll take a rain check."

She tried to move, but he refused to release her. "Is something wrong?" he asked.

Kyra decided that there was at least one definite setback to taking your best friend as a lover. He always knew when something was on your mind.

"Nope. Just thinking about a few things."

"Like that accounting error?"

She groaned. "No. But I am now."

She tried to tug her arm away. He used the momentum to haul her against him. "Hey, everything's going to be fine. You're going to find the error, make the needed adjustment, and everything will go back to being normal."

"You think so? Because I don't." She couldn't resist running her fingertip along his bottom lip. "You see, I already found the error. A three-hundred-dollar withdrawal for petty cash was increased to three thousand."

He grinned. "See. I told you you'd find it."

"Oh, yes, I found it. And the withdrawal slip has my name written all over it." She licked her lips, as a hum began in her lower stomach and quickly spread as she eyed his mouth. "Oh, don't worry. I'll find out whose mistake it is, because it's certainly not mine." She tilted her head, flicked her tongue over his chin then up to his lips. "By the way, I thought we might head over to your place tonight." She smiled at him. "I've always wondered what it would be like to have sex in that king-size sleigh bed of yours. And tonight's as good a time as any, don't you think?"

She watched his face for his response. And didn't like what she saw. His brows pulled together in a line and brackets appeared on either side of his delectable mouth. "I have a dinner appointment with the Nevilles tonight."

Uh-huh...

She shrugged. "So we'll do it after, then."

"I thought I'd just drop by here afterward."

"I see." She started to pull away.

"I've said something wrong, haven't I?"

She made a face. "Nope. Not a thing." She sniffed slightly. "I just find it curious that not once in the past week have we made it over to your place. While slowly but surely, you're stamping your presence all over my apartment."

"That's it? That's what's wrong?" He grinned and kissed her languidly. "What, you want me to take my toothbrush back?"

She playfully punched his shoulder. "Touch that toothbrush and you die."

"I'll leave the toothbrush."

"Good."

She returned his kiss with equal fervor then made a face. "Speaking of toothbrushes, big guy, it wouldn't hurt if you went a couple rounds with one."

He laughed and finally released her. "Ouch. Why didn't you warn me that you're the cruel type."

"Because you already knew."

Kyra turned and closed the door after herself then disappeared into the bedroom to get ready for work.

"I THINK it's absolutely disgraceful. Why you can see all the way to your..." the secretary lowered her voice and cupped a hand around her too chalky pink lips "...hoo-hoo."

Kyra stood gaping at Phyllis Kichler, who was sharing her daily critique of Kyra's new clothing. Her comments had grown more abrasive as the week went on. The difficult woman had always been a little antagonistic toward Kyra, but now she seemed to feel that she'd been granted special license to insult her, as well.

And just what in the world was a "hoo-hoo" anyway?

If it was what she thought it was, then Phyllis was doing her own share of hoo-hoo displaying. She wore her signature uniform of black polyester slacks and stretchy cotton top. The slacks had been tight on the older woman twenty pounds ago. Now...

Well, Kyra preferred not to go there. She didn't necessarily expect Phyllis to change her wardrobe. But she could buy the right size, for Pete's sake. No, a member of the fashion police Phyllis was not. But she was causing enough of a stir in the office to make Kyra dress down a bit. This morning Kyra's skirt was at least two whole inches longer, and her shirt had sleeves. Cute little cap sleeves that pulled the stretchy material tighter across her humble chest. She didn't have much, but what she did have, she realized she enjoyed showing.

"Well, thank you for sharing," Kyra said to the older woman, somehow managing a smile. "I'll make sure I see to the, um—" she capped her mouth with her own hand "—hoo-hoo problem right away." She straightened and caught herself tugging at her skirt. "Is Janet free? She left a note on my desk asking that I come see her."

Phyllis, though, seemed stuck on the hoo-hoo debate. She shook her head and practically snarled, "Back in my day, you would have been fired for wearing something so...sordid."

Back in her day Phyllis probably looked a whole lot like Kyra did. The sixties had been anything but conservative. In fact, much of Kyra's new wardrobe reflected the era.

But she didn't bother telling the secretary that, for fear that she'd never get out of the conversation.

Or that the woman might try firing her herself.

No. She had enough to contend with given Janet's hands-on interest in the recent accounting error.

"Janet?" Kyra said again, in case the secretary hadn't heard her the first time. "Is she free?"

Phyllis waved a hand. "Of course she's free. She's been waiting for you since she got in. Oh, and I'll have you know the fifteen minutes you were late didn't go without notice, either."

Kyra tried like hell not to make a face at the older woman and silently contemplated ways to poison the donuts that always sat on the corner of her desk.

"Come in, Kyra," Janet said without looking up from her desk.

Kyra did as asked. "Would you like me to close the door?"

Janet looked at her over her glasses. "I suppose that would be up to you."

Kyra glanced through the door at where Phyllis pretended to do filing, which put her right next to the open door.

Kyra closed it.

Janet sighed and slid her glasses off. Not for the first time, Kyra noticed how attractive the other woman was. Around the same age as Kyra, with silky straight jet-black hair and black eyes, Janet looked almost exactly like Salma Hayek. At least, when she smiled. Which, unfortunately, she didn't do often. In the four years since Kyra had signed on at the firm, if Janet wasn't barricaded in her office, she was traveling somewhere, drumming up business for the firm. In fact, Kyra realized that she knew very little personal information about the one female partner. Bryce Fisher was married with a toddler and had another baby on the way. Harvey Tanner was divorced and tried to fit in a personal life while making spousal and child support payments. And Michael... She caught herself smiling and coughed to clear her expression. Well, Michael she knew best of all.

Janet got up. "Please, have a seat." She walked to a carafe of coffee in the corner. "Would you like a cup?"

"I'd love some."

Janet wore a soft brown suit with a calf-length skirt and a high-necked silk shell. She smiled as she handed Kyra her coffee. "Black, right?"

"That's fine," Kyra said, although she preferred it with lots of sugar and cream. She took a sip and waited until Janet had reseated herself before saying, "So you came across the withdrawal slip."

Janet's eyes slightly widened. "Yes. Yes, I did."

"I didn't take out that much money." She put her cup on the edge of the desk. "I just thought I'd set the record straight before the conversation goes any further."

Janet sat back in her chair, tapping a nail against her cup. "I see. Then you must have some idea who did withdraw it, then."

"I'm still working on that."

"I see."

Kyra hated when people said that. Because it usually meant they were seeing something she wasn't.

"Is there anything else?" Kyra asked.

"I'm afraid there is," Janet said. "I've consulted with the firm's council on this matter and he's recommended that I bring in an outside source to monitor the investigation."

"Outside source.... Do you mean an auditor?" Kyra was aghast. Janet was bringing in someone from the outside?

Janet nodded. "Yes. Our attorney reassures me that this is merely a formality. It doesn't mean you're under suspicion for anything."

Which meant that she was.

Kyra suddenly wished she wasn't wearing high-heeled shoes because she was afraid she wouldn't be able to walk out of the office in them. And she didn't think taking them off and carrying them out would be a good idea, either.

"I see," she found herself saying.

But this time both of them knew exactly what she was seeing. And it wasn't pretty.

Janet smiled. "I'm sure this will all work out fine, Kyra."

Funny, isn't that what Michael had told her this morning?

"When can I expect the auditor?"

"This afternoon. And I trust you'll help him out as much as you can."

"Of course."

Kyra turned to leave.

"Oh, and I've already arranged for the auditor to do what it takes to investigate the matter. You'll, of course, stay with him while he does?"

Overtime.

"Of course."

Janet smiled. "Good."

9

MICHAEL CARRIED THE TRAY of food into the bedroom only to find Kyra fast asleep.

He grimaced and put the tray on the bedside table. It was midnight Saturday and she'd been working non-stop at the office with the auditor Janet had brought in, trying to get to the bottom of the accounting error. She'd stumbled into the apartment fifteen minutes ago, crawled into the shower then collapsed across the bed, her hair still wet, her delectable body wrapped in a towel.

Michael tugged at the damp terry cloth. He really should get her out of it before she caught a chill. He pulled a flap back from her clean, pink skin and immediately felt desire careen through his groin. Okay, maybe that wasn't such a good idea.

Maybe if he put something on her first...

He searched through her drawers for something as unattractive as possible. Something that would help him tuck her in without succumbing to the temptation to wake her so they might continue their sexual explorations. He discovered that Kyra's new interest in sexy clothes extended to her evening wear, as well. Either that or she'd always had a naughty side she'd kept hidden under her conservative clothing. Sliding the drawer closed, he opted for one of his work shirts instead, grabbing it from where it was draped across the back of a chair. He carefully slid the sleeves up her arms then pulled the shirt together over her chest, buttoning it as best he could, given that he couldn't pull the back down.

There. He could handle this now. He reached under the hem of the shirt and tugged on the towel, sliding it from under her boneless body.

That accomplished, he sat next to her on the mattress and lightly swept her wispy hair back from her face. Dear, sweet Kyra.

He frowned. That was the first time he'd thought of her in that way since they'd made the transition from friends to lovers. For the past week she'd been va-va-voom Kyra, capable of shocking him and rocking his world in a way it had never been rocked before. But now with her sleeping, her brow still creased from where she'd been worrying so much lately, he couldn't help but feel his original fondness for her return. It not only returned, but it began to mingle with the ceaseless desire he felt for the woman lying oblivious to his thoughts, the two emotions complementing each other.

She was an incredible woman, Kyra. Strong and competent and sexy as hell. Strong and competent he'd always known about. Sexy was a recent but potent discovery. He couldn't remember a time when he'd had so much sex in such a short period of time. And if she was conscious, they'd probably be setting the sheets on fire yet again tonight.

Mr. Tibbs jumped on the bed and eyed Kyra, then looked up at Michael accusingly.

"What? I didn't do anything." Although he found himself wishing she was exhausted because of him instead of what was going on at work.

Mr. Tibbs plopped his overfed furry butt down on the sheet.

"Are you hungry?" Michael asked, deciding that now was as good a time as any to come to a truce with the scruffy feline that seemed to merely tolerate his presence.

He picked up a piece of cubed ham and held it out. Mr. Tibbs eyed him, then sniffed experimentally. Then he bit the piece of meat along with Michael's thumb and leaped off the bed.

Michael shook his hand, then examined the damage. Nothing he wouldn't recover from. Still, any truce with the jealous cat was off for the time being.

His gaze was drawn back to Kyra's sleeping face. Without a lick of the makeup she'd taken to wearing lately, it was easy to imagine the woman he once knew. The one that had been his best friend.

To go or to stay. That was the question.

When he realized that Kyra was going to be at the office all day, he saw to errands, then checked in at the firm himself after six that night to finalize the plans for the Neville house. The outside auditor had made it impossible for any hanky-panky. Not that he thought Kyra was up to any anyway. She'd looked completely drained. And she had been, if her current state was anything to go by. At eleven-thirty he'd finally convinced her to close up shop and come home with him. For some strange reason, she'd seemed surprised that he'd driven to her place. Then a little disappointed. He'd wanted to talk to her about that. But it didn't appear they were going to be talking or much of anything now.

He ran a fingertip down her check then over her jawline. He didn't know if he had the strength to leave her and go back to his condo. But staying with her like this, feeling all warm and fuzzy inside, posed a problem, as well. He wasn't exactly sure why, but he didn't know if it was wise to allow his feelings for her to mingle with his desire. Up until now, they both seemed to do a pretty good job of keeping both relationships—friends and lovers—separate. And he'd like to continue to do that. If only because he didn't have the courage to think about doing anything else.

Just more than a week had passed since she'd seduced him with pizza and an ice-blue nightie. In the dark recesses of his mind, sometimes he swore he could hear a clock ticking. A timer of sorts, counting down the minutes when Kyra would wake up and do away with him as she had with so many other men in her life. He didn't want to think that way, but he was a practical man who knew how to examine all the angles. And the thought that Kyra might wake up one morning, look at him, and decide they were done...well, it loomed a very strong possibility, indeed.

And frankly, the inevitability was beginning to scare the living shit out of him.

Go home. That's what he should do. Just get up from the bed, gather his things, and head back to his condo for the night. He'd leave her a note saying he'd be back in the morning to take her to the firm, where they'd left her car.

He moved at the same time Kyra whispered something in her sleep and rolled toward him, sliding her delicate hand across his abdomen then humming in content.

Michael swallowed hard, looking at where her purple-painted nails were mere millimeters from the waist of his pants and his arousal.

Okay, he could handle this. They would just sleep together. Sleep. He wouldn't think beyond those terms. He'd stretch out next to her and catch some shut-eye and in the morning he'd discover that nothing had changed.

He gently shifted her and stretched out, deciding to leave his jeans and T-shirt on.

Michael shut off the light and took a deep breath. Once he was settled against the pillows, Kyra curled up against him and hummed again.

Uh-oh...

KYRA REMOVED HER HEAD from where she had it propped up against her hand and glanced to where the auditor was removing a long line of tape from the manual calculator behind her. He stared at her forehead. Great, she probably had palm head. Which would be fine if that's all she had. Truth was, she was tired as hell. When she'd woken up at six that morning to find Michael's arms cradling her, his chin resting on the top of her head, she'd wanted nothing more than to cuddle closer and fall back asleep. Instead she'd called a taxi and had come to the firm to find the auditor already there.

That was five hours ago.

"Done?" she asked.

The auditor's name was Walter Westheimer and she'd bet dollars to donuts he'd once worked at the IRS. He looked like the type who would get into taking hardworking families' houses away. Oh, he was probably only a few years older than her, and attractive enough, with his blond hair and blue eyes. But there was something...ruthless about the way he tapped away on the calculator he'd brought along with him every morning and took home with him every night. It made her skin crawl. She liked being a bookkeeper, but it wasn't exactly her life. She had the sensation that Westheimer dreamed about numbers when he slept.

"Done," he finally said, folding the calculator tape, then stapling it in place.

Kyra swiveled her chair around to face where he'd set up shop on the worktable behind her. "And?"

"And nothing. I can't come to any conclusions until I get the actual withdrawal slip from the bank tomorrow."

"Of course." Kyra frowned, then looked at her watch. She'd tried calling Michael earlier, but had gotten his cell phone voice mail. He had yet to call back. "It's lunchtime. Do you want to go catch a bite?"

Walter looked at her as if she'd just suggested they strip naked and have sex on her computer.

"Then again, maybe not," she said, resisting the urge to roll her eyes.

Where had Janet found this guy?

Walter placed his things in his briefcase, then stood and extended his hand to her. "Thank you for your help in this matter. I'll be sure to pass on your cooperation to your employer."

Kyra hesitantly took his hand. "Did you expect anything less?" She dropped her hand. "So I'll see you tomorrow morning, then?"

He picked up his briefcase. "I'll be tendering my findings directly to your employer. I suggest you speak with her."

Kyra stared at him, trying to figure out if he was being purposely ominous or whether it was just part of his demeanor.

She decided it was his demeanor. She hadn't done anything wrong. Any investigation was sure to prove that out.

He left her office without another word, then she heard the outer door close behind him. She flopped back in her chair and considered the mess they'd both made. She really should make a dent in cleaning it up.

Instead, she picked up the phone and called Michael again.

He answered on the third ring. "Hello?" he said quietly.

"*¡Hola, amigo!*" she said, trying to inject humor into her voice. "You up for some lunch? I'm starving. I was thinking that little place out by the marina. You know, the seafood place?"

"Can you hold on a minute?"

Kyra pulled back, surprised. "Sure."

A moment later he was back. "I can't do lunch with you, Kyra."

"Where are you?"

"It's the last Sunday of the month."

She tried to make sense out of his words. "I don't...oh, wait." She blew out a long breath. "Dinner at your parents', right? I'm sorry. I forgot."

And he'd obviously forgotten to mention it to her.

"I was going to leave you a note this morning, but you left before I did."

And she hadn't left a note.

God, this was awkward.

"What time do you think you'll be home later?" Michael asked.

"Actually, I'll be home in a half hour." She let out another long breath thinking she might as well tackle some of the refiling while she was there. "The auditor just finished. He's going to give Janet his findings tomorrow."

"Good, so everything's worked out then."

She bit her bottom lip. He seemed so confident in her. She wished she could feel as sure. "Yes, I guess." She swiveled in her chair and fished around for one of the energy bars she usually kept in her purse. "So, about tonight, then. I thought maybe we could meet at your place."

Out of the frying pan, into the fire.

Kyra hadn't realized she was going to make the suggestion until it was out of her mouth. But the fact that they were at her apartment all the time was beginning to bug her. She didn't think Michael was hiding anything from her, but surely, there had to be a reason why he was avoiding taking her home with him.

"Okay," he said hesitantly. "What time?"

She glanced at her watch even though she already knew the time. "Say six? Is that too early for you?"

"I was thinking too late."

She caught the sexy innuendo in his voice and smiled. "I could meet you there in an hour."

There was a voice on the other end of the line and Michael responded to it. "Six o'clock, then?"

"Hmm. Six."

Kyra broke the connection, then concentrated on finding the energy bar. There. She examined the wrapper that was a little worse for wear and checked the expiration date. A week from today. She was safe. She tore open the end with her teeth and dug into it, trying like hell to ignore the uneasiness she felt about everything in her life at the moment. First there was the inexplicable accounting error. Then she'd had to deal with the auditor. And now Michael was at his parents', without having said word one about her possibly going with him.

She'd met Conchita and Antonio Romero once, at the wedding of one of Michael's cousins. He'd been short a date and she'd filled in at the last minute. They'd seemed like nice enough people. Not that she'd had a chance to really talk to them. Whenever they came within speaking distance, Michael had whisked her away, claiming he was saving her from the "marriage talk" they gave all of his dates.

She chewed...and chewed...and chewed, trying not to think that the concoction of nuts and—she read the wrapper—caramel tasted like cardboard.

Okay, so after a week of hot sex, Michael wasn't exactly ready to take her to his parents' for dinner. Since she didn't have much of a family to compare the situation to she couldn't say whether that was normal or not. But she would liked to have made the decision herself. He could have asked, and she could have refused.

Although she probably wouldn't have. Michael had talked about what a good cook his mother was.

Crumbs fell to her skirt and Kyra pushed her chair back to sweep them off the short black leather. Mid-sweep, her hand slowed and she stared at the sexy scrap of material that didn't leave a whole lot to the imagination, then followed it up to her low-cut tank top. The energy bar seemed to lodge in her throat. Could Michael be ashamed of her?

She remembered his initial reaction to her transformation. His comparing her to a twenty-dollar streetwalker. She pulled the wastebasket from under her desk and spit the mouthful she was chewing out, not trusting her capabilities to swallow it. If that's what Michael had thought, what would his parents think?

She groaned then tossed the rest of the bar into the wastebasket, as well.

Good enough to fool around with, but not to take home to mom. Was that it?

She made a face. What was she thinking? This was Michael she was talking about. Yes, while his relationship with his parents was…well, difficult, to hear him explain it, he would never scheme to keep them from seeing her. In all likelihood, he was probably trying to save her from dealing with them.

The problem was that she'd love the opportunity to get to know them.

She glanced at her watch. There were hours to go before six. She eyed the mountain of files and decided that there was nothing better to do to help the time go by.

MICHAEL PUSHED RICE around his plate. Mealtime with his parents was always silent. He'd been taught that conversation was best left for when everyone had finished eating. Silverware clinking against china, and ice cubes melting in glasses were the only sounds in the formal dining room where his mother always set out dinner, even though there was only the three of them. Michael had always secretly yearned for them to eat together in the kitchen just once to see what it was like. But his parents seemed to like the formality of the meal.

"So, who was that on the phone?" his father asked.

Michael blinked at his still-full plate then over to where his father was placing his linen napkin next to his on the table. Michael cleared his throat then smoothed his tie. Another family tradition was dressing for the meal. Of course his mother always went to church on Sunday, but Michael and his father were still required to dress up, regardless.

"Kyra."

His parents looked at each other.

"You remember Kyra? I brought her to Nina's wedding. She has long brown hair...." *Had* long brown hair. "She's a friend."

He cringed the minute the words left his mouth.

"Friend" didn't come close to describing his relationship with Kyra lately. But he wasn't quite sure how to go about classifying it. Intimate friends? Best friends with benefits? He frowned and followed his father's lead by placing his napkin next to his plate.

"Oh, yes, I remember her," his mother said in her accented voice. She smiled. "She is a nice girl, no?"

Michael nodded, not about to share how very nice— or how very naughty—she really was.

"You should bring her to dinner next month," his father announced.

Michael coughed, nearly choking on the water he was drinking. "I don't know if that's such a good idea."

"Why not?" his mother asked.

Why not, indeed?

Michael rubbed his forehead. "She works on Sundays," he lied, cringing again. He'd never lied to his parents. He'd stretched the truth on occasion. Challenged them more frequently. But he had never lied to them.

Which left him to wonder why he was lying now. He was thirty-three years old, for God's sake. He didn't have to lie about anything. Especially when he'd probably get caught if his relationship with Kyra stretched to beyond tomorrow.

Perhaps it was because he didn't truly believe that it would. Everything was too...strange. Too new. Too... mind-blowing.

"So we'll move dinner to Saturday, then," his mother said. "In fact, there's no need to wait until next month. We can have dinner this Saturday. Or the following one, if that's too soon for you."

A year from now was too soon for Michael, but he didn't dare say that.

He considered telling them that Kyra worked Saturdays, too, but knew that would only result in another alternate date.

"I, um, I'll ask her," he said, though he had no intention of doing any such thing.

Aside from his own confusion regarding his relationship with Kyra, he didn't think his parents and his...lover would get on so well. Not given Kyra's recent transformation.

Conchita and Antonio had come to Florida—his mother by herself as a teenager, his father with his family when he was eight—and they'd made it their mission to fit into polite American society. Michael thought that their being of different heritage—his mother from Peru, his father from Spain—made that desire doubly strong. They'd worked hard to build a solid foundation in the restaurant-supply business, adopted American traditions and taught their only child how to be an American. Only, Michael grew up thinking his parents didn't have a clue of what an American was. An American wasn't a state of learning; it was a way of being.

Of course, he'd never tell them that. But he knew what they considered acceptable behavior. And, well, Kyra would not be acceptable in their eyes. She would be pointed at as an example of what was wrong with America and its many temptations for excess.

His mother said something to his father about having seen an old friend at the cathedral and the two warmly talked about the reunion, discussing the possibility of inviting the man and his wife over for dinner.

Michael caught himself glancing at his watch for the fourth time in as many minutes. He always stayed through till coffee after dessert. But all he could think about was Kyra getting home about now and how much he wanted to be there with her.

He pushed away from the table. "I'm sorry, but I've got to go."

"Go?" His mother rose, a concerned frown creasing her forehead.

"Nonsense. You haven't had dessert yet," his father said.

Michael looked at his watch. "I just remembered I promised to meet a client this afternoon."

"Michael," his father said in a voice that brooked no argument.

Michael was going to argue.

"Sorry, Dad. Mom, dinner was wonderful." He started for the door, then turned. "I love you both."

The words, so simple, had rarely been said in their household. And they dumbfounded his parents.

With a simple, awkward wave, he opened the door and left.

COME OVER *when you get home.*

Kyra read the note taped to her door, her heart doing a triple beat before settling into a steady, thrumming rhythm.

She didn't have to ask who the note was from. Even though Michael hadn't signed it, she'd recognize his handwriting anywhere. He must have left his parents right after she talked to him two hours ago. Maybe he'd dropped by, hoping to see her, and when she wasn't here, had decided to leave a note.

"I hope you don't plan on having company up there tonight!" Mrs. Kaminsky screamed up the stairwell.

Kyra waved the note. "Not to worry, Mrs. K. I'm going out tonight."

The older woman sniffed then headed back toward her door. "Just make sure you're quiet when you come home. An old woman like myself needs her beauty sleep!"

She slammed her apartment door, leaving Kyra smiling stupidly as she watched after her.

KYRA LOOKED like every man's version of a walking wet dream. Covered from breast to upper thigh in shiny red—was that plastic? Or rubber? Michael stood holding the door to his apartment open and nearly groaned. It didn't matter what the material was. It looked like her sexy body had been vacuum-packed... and he couldn't wait to peel away the wrapping to free the fresh flesh waiting inside.

"Um, hi."

Michael realized that he hadn't looked into Kyra's face since answering her knock. He did so now. And felt his stomach pitch to his feet at the anxious expression she wore.

Uh-oh...

He held the door open. "Come on in."

She hesitated, then slowly stepped into the nicely designed two-floor condo, her gaze darting around the room.

"Everything okay?" he asked, closing the door.

She nodded, causing her blond spiky hair to quiver. "Um, yeah. You?"

Despite her obvious discomfort, Michael found himself grinning.

He'd rarely known Kyra to be uncomfortable in any surroundings. Especially not this bursting-at-the-seams version of her. But she definitely seemed ill at ease.

"I'm fine," he said, chiseling his gaze from her plump backside and clearing his throat. "Would you like some wine? Why don't you go into the living room while I go get us some?"

"Okay."

She didn't move. Instead, Michael was forced to inch his way around her, his breath catching as he brushed up against that slippery dress she was wearing.

Maybe he wouldn't take the dress off. Maybe he'd

leave it on and bend her over the couch and watch how it shimmered when he rocked into her...

His pace quickened. At the rate he was going, they wouldn't make it to dinner, much less all the rest of the things he had planned for the evening.

Earlier in the day, sometime before his mother's inviting Kyra over for dinner and his father's attempt to get him to stay, he realized that he was incapable of holding back anymore. No matter what path Kyra had mapped out for them, he could do nothing less than give this relationship his all. He did it in his career. And now he found himself needing to do it with Kyra.

Come what may, he was in this for the long haul....

10

Section III:
Letting the kitten roar

COME ON, *you've been here before,* her little voice whispered. *Why are you so nervous?* She swallowed hard. What did it mean when even your inner voice whispered?

She slowly stepped into the modern living room with its vaulted ceiling, stone fireplace and gleaming wood beams and thought that it meant she was in big trouble.

Ever since getting Michael's note, she'd been looking forward to tonight. Until she was on her way over and wondered if the new dress she'd bought especially for the occasion was overkill, wondered if she'd been off base thinking that Michael had purposely avoided inviting her over. Or, worse, that she'd been target-on.

She squeezed her eyes shut and tossed her purse onto the beige leather couch. The same couch she'd sat on countless times catching the latest video with Michael, playing a Scrabble game, or just enjoying his latest CD. Now she eyed it as if she didn't know what it was meant for.

She looked around the room as if seeing it for the first time.

She knew that he'd designed the subdivision of condos, full units that were more like houses but for the connection they shared with a neighbor. Each unit was unique both inside and out, without costing a single penny more due to Michael's ingenious idea of taking the same materials and making them different. The contractor hadn't been so smart, though. He'd come up short on cash and couldn't obtain more financing. Michael had claimed one of the condos as his own rather than take the guy to court.

She glanced down at her watch, then craned her neck to try to see into the hallway. What was taking him so long? If he didn't come back soon, she swore she'd jump out of her skin.

Speaking of skin...

She glanced down at her dress, caught off guard by the brightness of it. She shimmied her hips a little, watching the light play against the shiny plastic. Already the skin that was in contact with the dress was moist with sweat. The shop girl had told her to be careful while wearing it or she was liable to lose enough weight in one night that the suffocating material might slide right off her.

"Enjoying yourself?"

Kyra snapped her head up and stared at where Michael held a bottle and two wineglasses in one hand, a tray in the other. She caught herself giggling nervously and stopped. "It's something, isn't it?"

He strode into the room and placed the items he held on the coffee table. "An entity unto itself, definitely."

Her smile vanished. "You don't like it?"

His gaze moved over the dress but lingered on her exposed flesh longer. "I love it."

Kyra felt her skin grow hot as she watched his pupils get larger in his already dark eyes.

God, but he was one of the most strikingly handsome men she'd ever seen. At times like these, when he was looking at her as if he only had her on his mind, he stole her breath away. Of course, she'd always thought he was good-looking, but somehow, early on in their friendship, she'd managed to secure a pair of blinders, putting him off-limits, and making looking at him the way she was now forbidden.

"Is red okay?"

"Red?" she asked, wondering if he was talking about her dress.

"Wine."

"Oh. Yes. Of course."

She lifted a glass and watched as he filled it then his own. She placed it against her lips, but for some odd reason, couldn't seem to make herself drink from it. She smiled, noticing Michael watched her. "Um, what's the occasion?"

He shook his head. "There isn't one."

She looked down into her glass. "At my place, you get directions to the refrigerator," she said.

"Yes, well, wait till you see what I've cooked up for dinner."

"You cooked?"

"Mmm, hmm."

Okay, forget jumping out of her skin. She was going to run for the door.

Michael had never once, in the four years that she'd known him, cooked for her. Sure, he'd put together sandwiches, opened a bag of pretzels, ordered in pizza, but that didn't count. She did all that, too.

Her level of anxiety edged up a couple notches.

Then it hit her. This new view she was getting of Michael. He was treating her as he might treat one of his dates.

She was both flattered…and oddly bothered. The flattered part quickly retreated, leaving her strictly bothered. She knew the type of women Michael usually dated. Tall, sleek, sophisticated ones that would know the difference between merlot and chardonnay.

She didn't realize how different "date material" Michael was from "her friend" Michael. Her friend Michael would have asked her what toppings she wanted on her pizza, handed her a beer and they would have been done with it.

She wasn't entirely sure what to do with this Michael.

He raised his glass. "Here's to your clearing things up at work."

Kyra stared at him, then realized some action was required from her. "Oh." She lifted her glass, too, and he clinked his against hers. "Amen."

This time when she put the glass to her lips, she chugged half of it down. When she finally put the glass down, she smiled at Michael's puzzled expression.

"Something is wrong," he said, putting his glass down next to hers.

She cleared her throat. "No…not wrong, exactly. I know this is going to sound silly, but…"

"What?"

"This all feels…strange, somehow."

"Strange good? Or strange bad?"

She shrugged. "I'm not exactly sure yet." She looked

toward the hall. She smelled something cooking and wrinkled her nose. "You've never treated me like this."

He grinned. "I know. I was thinking maybe it was time I started."

"Why?"

He blinked at her, appearing genuinely surprised. "Because I think you deserve to be treated special."

Rats. Now she felt guilty. Here she thought he was treating her like every other woman in his life, and he thought he was doing something special for her. She picked up her glass again. "I thought the way you were treating me before was pretty special."

She chanced a glance at him and found him wearing a sexy grin. "How? By keeping you in bed?"

She returned the smile. "Well...yes."

Something dinged in the other room. "I'd better go see to that. I wouldn't want the first dinner I ever cook you to burn."

Kyra watched him leave then sighed and put the glass back down on the table. "I'd much rather something else burn. Like the two of us." She scooped up a handful of crackers then headed toward the balcony doors. It took her a few moments, but she finally figured out how to unlock them. Then, opening them, she stepped from the cool condo into the thick, sultry Florida air. She shivered and moved toward the railing that overlooked the Gulf. She hadn't paid much attention to the view he had from his condo before. Now she took a deep breath, watched a pelican dive into the white-capped waves, and smiled at the feel of the slanting sun kissing her skin.

"Would you like to eat out here?"

She heard Michael's voice behind her and wanted to

tell him that she wasn't really hungry. But that wouldn't be fair. She turned and leaned against the railing. "Whatever you like."

His smile wavered. "Okay."

She looked him over, from shiny loafers and pressed dark slacks to crisp silk shirt. He'd rolled the sleeves up his forearms and the top buttons were undone on his shirt, revealing a few soft, dark curls. He looked good enough to eat. And distant enough to be out of reach.

He came to stand next to her, looking out onto the Gulf of Mexico. "When I first moved in here, I loved the view. Most times now, I even forget that this is out here."

Kyra turned to look out onto the water with him. "I was just thinking the same thing. You know, about when I come over."

Those times seemed so long ago and far away, although she'd just been over there two weeks ago. It wasn't time that separated then from now, but perspective. And she wasn't sure she was adjusting all that well to her new outlook. She glanced at Michael, taking in his strong profile, the way he squinted against the sun without worrying about wrinkles.

"I take it this isn't how you envisioned tonight going," he said quietly.

She looked down and laughed softly. "No. I guess it isn't."

His gaze was intense when he turned to her. "Would you have felt better if I'd attacked you the instant you walked in the door?"

She automatically reached out and hooked her finger inside the top of his shirt, the hair there tickling her skin. "Yes. I guess I would have."

"My parents asked you over for dinner."

Kyra looked at him. "What?"

"You know, dinner. My mother thought it might be a good idea if I brought you by."

"You told them about us?"

He averted his gaze. "No. But I think they must have picked up on something." He shrugged and clasped his hands together against the railing. "I didn't quite know what to say, you know? Not about the dinner part. Of course, I'd like to take you over there. But I didn't know how to classify our relationship."

She removed her finger and stood beside him, leaning against the railing, too. "That makes two of us." She tucked her short hair behind her ear. Not that it was long enough to do that, but it felt reassuring to do it anyway. "Mrs. K. says she knows no friends that carry on the way we do."

"Did she break your eardrums while saying it?"

"Nearly. It's a good thing there are only the two apartments there, or else the whole neighborhood might have heard."

"And would that be bad?"

"What? The neighbors hearing?"

"No. The neighbors knowing about us."

"Ah." She gazed over the side of the balcony to the green grass below. "I don't know. What do you think?"

"I don't know."

She looked at him a long moment, suddenly feeling as if he was looking for something, something he was afraid she might not give him.

"Ask me," she said.

"Pardon me?"

She lightly hit him on the arm with a loose fist. "Don't give me that 'pardon me' stuff. The Michael I know would have said 'what.'"

He chuckled. "The Michael you've come to know would have stripped you out of that wrapper the instant he saw you."

"Then there's that."

He lifted his hand to rest at the back of her neck. She was instantly aware of his skin against hers, tiny shivers trailing down her spine then back up again. "Okay, so then I'll just come out and ask you."

She began to stiffen, but he started making little circles at the nape of her neck.

"Have you thought about where all this is going?" He stared intently at her. "You. Me. Whatever's happening between us?"

MICHAEL WATCHED myriad emotions play over Kyra's beautiful face. The evening sun cast her skin aglow and heightened the shadow of her eyes.

He didn't realize how important her answer was to him until he asked the question. It was all he could do not to freeze up, to continue massaging her neck as he waited for her response.

"Have I thought about where this is going...." she repeated before looking back out at the water.

Michael fought the desire to make her face him. To answer him directly.

"Um, I guess I have. A little."

Relief rushed through his body like an elixir. "Good."

She leaned into him. "I have to admit, though, that I really thought you were purposely keeping me away from your place. You know, after the change in our friendship."

She looked at him.

"Like you were trying to keep a part of yourself closed off from me."

He grimaced. "I think it's because I was."

She lifted an eyebrow and he ran his other hand through his hair. "I don't know. I think the word you used earlier—strange, wasn't it?—is exactly how I'd describe the way I've been feeling lately. Sometimes I think things are moving too fast. Other times not fast enough."

She nodded and ran her fingertips over his forearm.

"Sometimes I want to forget about the sex and ask my best friend a question. But most times I want to forget the questions and go for the sex."

"And now?" she asked, her voice low and husky. "What are you feeling right this minute?"

He skimmed her provocative expression, then dropped his gaze down to where her small breasts pressed against the shiny fabric of her dress. "Right now I want to say 'to hell with dinner' and put that chaise longue behind you to work."

Her lips turned up into a suggestive smile. "So let's hurry up and eat dinner, then we can check out the chaise."

He tightened his fingers on her neck then tugged her closer. Her breath was hot on his face as he considered her for a long moment, then pressed his mouth against hers for a lingering kiss. "Sounds like a plan to me."

IT WAS ONLY when Michael was filling her to overflowing, his thick flesh pulsing inside her, his hips pressed against hers, that Kyra felt all doubt leave.

As she fought to catch her breath, she pressed her mouth against his shoulder, lapping the salt from his hot skin, seemingly unable to get enough. As agreed, they'd gone inside to eat the dinner he'd prepared. If she'd felt a little uncomfortable sitting at his dining-room table, a linen napkin in her lap when she was used to holding a paper one, looking at the meal that was almost too pretty to eat, she promised herself that she wouldn't let Michael know that. He'd obviously worked hard to impress her. If he only knew how very impressed she was already. He was a man as determined in his personal life as he was in his professional one.

He'd prepared dessert, as well. But Kyra had had another kind of dessert in mind. So she'd taken him by the hand and led him back out to the balcony, slipping out of her clothes as she went. Then they'd begun the evening's extracurricular activities on the chaise longue, the sunset bathing them in a warm yellow glow, turning Michael into an Aztec god as he strained above her, his face a work of wonder as he drove into her again and again.

That was four hours ago, and aside from a brief bathroom break they'd been going at it ever since.

Kyra kept waiting for the sheer passion that took hold of her every time Michael touched her to pass. Expected to open her eyes and find her need of him lessened by half. Instead she found she wanted him more and more each time they made love. Even after she'd passed the point where she couldn't physically go on, she wanted him again. And that hadn't altered a bit with the change in venue. It didn't matter whether they were at her apartment on her old, squeaky mattress, at work on top of his drafting table, or here in his designer king-size bed with the monochromatic linens.

She closed her eyes and dug her fingers into his arms. In fact, tonight their lovemaking seemed to be better than ever, more intense somehow. No, Michael was more intense. His strokes long and controlled, his gaze hotter. And she didn't think it was only because they were at his place. Something seemed to have shifted in his feelings for her. Something she couldn't put a finger on but dearly wanted to.

"Carbs. I need carbs," Michael murmured against her skin then closed his mouth over her shoulder.

"Ouch," she softly protested, arching up against him as he gently bit into her flesh. "Nothing but pure protein there."

He chuckled then kissed her. And kissed her again.

Kyra licked her lips, disappointed when he withdrew and climbed from the bed, rolling the used condom into a wad of tissue, then tossing it into a nearby wastebasket.

She lifted herself up on her elbows. "Where are you going?"

"To get that dessert we passed up earlier."

"I thought we just had dessert."

He grinned at her and padded from the room.

Kyra collapsed back to the mattress, feeling gloriously well loved. She stretched her hands above her head then flexed her toes, brilliantly aware of every single muscle in her body.

What was she thinking, that she wanted to get inside

Michael's head? She couldn't recognize the thoughts, the feelings, streaming through her own mind. She was so ill equipped to translate the messages there. A card-carrying serial dater, she had never come close to having what she now shared with Michael. Nothing with which to draw parallels, to point to and say, "That's it. That's the reason I feel the way I do," and map out the rest of the story.

Rather, the story seemed to be mapping out its own route and she was helpless to do anything more than watch...and follow.

The prospect both excited and terrified her. While she relished the highs of the ride, the white-hot heat of ecstasy and phenomenal orgasms, she loathed the lows that went with it. The dark periods of self-doubt. Of feeling so insecure, she questioned things she had been fanatically sure about mere moments before.

"Ready?"

No, her mind screamed.

She opened her eyes to watch Michael walk into the room in all his naked glory, his erection standing clear and proud and strong against his stomach, his eyes smiling at her as he placed a chocolate feast beside her on the bed.

She groaned, allowing him to hand-feed her a truffle that was absolutely out of this world.

She allowed the sweet chocolate to dissolve on her tongue then slowly chewed, relishing every sensation, exploring every texture. She hummed and closed her eyes again, unmotivated to move a muscle. "Tell me you didn't make this."

"I didn't make it."

She cracked her eyelids to peer out at him.

He grinned. "Desserts I don't do. I got all this at a pastry shop just outside the subdivision."

He fed her another piece of chocolate, this one flavored with cherries. "Good," she said, wiping runaway saliva with the back of her hand. "Because if you had made all this, I'd definitely start to wonder."

"About my sexuality?"

She giggled.

"You're sexist."

"And you're cruel."

She somehow managed to turn onto her side and prop herself up on her elbow. He sat half-turned next to her on the mattress, his musky arousal mere inches from the tray.

"Why?" he asked, eating a square of dark chocolate. "Because I'm replacing all the calories you just burned?"

Her gaze followed the jagged blue vein that pulsed along the length of his erection, her mouth watering for an entirely different reason. "Then there's that."

She dipped her finger into a small white bowl that held what looked like chocolate syrup, then stuck it into her mouth. Definitely chocolate syrup. She glanced up into Michael's face to find his eyes dark with lust. "It's for the tangerine pieces."

"Well, the tangerine pieces are just going to have to find their own chocolate, because something else is just begging for this."

She picked up the small bowl and positioned it over the top of his erection. Then with the utmost care, she tipped it, allowing chocolate to drizzle over the taut knob, then down over the side, following the line of the vein. Kyra licked her lips then bent forward to run her tongue along the outside of that vein.

Michael groaned. "No carbs there," he murmured.

She smiled up at him even as she continued to run the tip of her tongue along his thick shaft. "Nope. Pure protein."

She fit her lips over the top, swirling her tongue around the ridge then dipping it into the eye winking at her from the top. The proof of his arousal beaded there and she licked it off. Languidly, she moved a hand to cup his swollen sac, gently squeezing, then wrapped her fingers around his throbbing stem. She fastened her mouth over him again, this time applying suction.

Michael groaned and his hips bucked against her, nearly toppling over the tray.

"Kyra," he whispered in husky warning.

She blinked up at him, feigning innocence. "What?"

"In about two seconds, you're going to get a whole different kind of syrup."

"Oh?" She licked her lips as if savoring the thought. "Is it good?"

She picked up the bowl again and dribbled the remainder of the chocolate syrup over his pulsing flesh, then set about meticulously cleaning it off, sucking, then licking, then sucking again.

There was something powerfully provocative about holding him in her mouth. About giving to him, pleasuring him, that made her so hot her own thighs dampened. She gasped when he plucked at one of her nipples. She applied even more suction, having removed every drop of chocolate and was now going for the grand prize.

Michael's low, drawn-out moan filled the air, alerting her to how very close he was to climax. She took him in as far as she could and began working her hand on the lower part of his shaft. Up and down, up and down, quickening the rhythm of her hand and her mouth.

She felt his fingers between her legs. She opened her thighs, allowing him access to her slick core, where he immediately found her tight, quivering bit of flesh and squeezed at the same time he climaxed, pulling Kyra right along with him.

Kyra swallowed and swallowed, trying to take in every drop of him as he filled her mouth, even as her own muscles contracted in sweet agony.

Finally the hot stream dissipated and she licked him clean, her gaze fastened on his face, watching him.

Michael smoothed her short hair back and grinned. "You know, I'll never be able to eat chocolate again without getting a hard-on."

She stretched out beside him then closed her eyes and smiled. "Good." She may have sounded nonchalant, but it touched her to know that she had created a memory for both of them that wouldn't dim with the morning light.

She felt something against her lips. She opened them without opening her eyes at the same time she opened her legs for Michael's other hand. He popped another piece of chocolate into her mouth, then slid two fingers deep inside her flesh.

She gasped and arched her back.

"So hot...so wet," she heard him murmur, the sound of his approval as much of a turn-on as his fingers.

He slowly removed his fingers, giving her clit a little

tweak as he did so. She moved to protest but he instantly placed more chocolate in her mouth. She hummed as she chewed, then moaned when his fingers were replaced by something ultimately more satisfying....

11

"IT'S CALLED LOVE, stupid."

The following day Kyra lay back on her sofa, absently patting Mr. Tibbs as the morning sun slanted through her front window and bathed her feet in warmth. She'd left Michael's condo at about six o'clock, needing to get home to shower and change for work. She was ready. At least physically. But emotionally she needed a little no-nonsense counseling. And her sister Alannah had always been good at doling that out.

Well, at least she used to be. Still officially in the honeymoon stages of her own relationship, her sister sounded...well, not much like her usual, practical sister.

"Gasp. You just used the ultimate of four-letter words," Kyra joked. She nudged Mr. T. from her lap and sat up, not wanting to crease her skirt and blouse any more than she already had. She'd settled on the leopard-print skirt, a frilly black bra and a sheer white blouse that didn't hide a thing. "No, seriously. I need for you to tell me what to do, Al. I mean, Michael's my best friend. He's been that for four years. And now he's the best damn lover I've ever had." She sighed and straightened a knickknack on her coffee table that didn't need straightening. She moved it back. "What should I do?"

"Marry him."

Kyra jumped up from the sofa so fast, she nearly tripped.

"I'm serious, Kyra," Alannah said, conviction in her voice. "You're telling me all this as if it's some sort of problem, when it sounds to me like you've found your soul mate."

Kyra stared at the phone. "Have you gone soft in the head?" She knocked the receiver against the table, then put it back to her ear. "Did I really just hear you use the words soul mate? Holy cow, Al, you're an inch away from my coming up there to make sure Ben hasn't brainwashed you."

Her sister's soft laugh made her smile.

It had been so very long since she'd heard her sister so happy. In fact, she was sure she hadn't heard Alannah laugh so much in her life. She knew it was because there had been so little to laugh about when they were growing up. While Kyra couldn't remember the incident that left them orphans, Alannah recalled every detail. Not only recalled it, but relived it constantly. Or at least she had until she'd finally given in to Ben's demand that their annual tryst over the past four years either become something more concrete or end altogether.

They'd gotten married three months ago.

"You know," Alannah said quietly. "I'm not convinced that you've emerged from our childhood as unscathed as you'd have me think."

Kyra made a face. Despite the physical distance that separated them, she and her sister still had an emotional link that was downright eerie sometimes.

"Pooh," she said, but with only half the conviction she wanted to.

"Think about it, Kyra. Every time I talk to you, you're going out with a different guy. The only constant man in your life has been Michael. And now you're sure that something has to be wrong even there. I'm sensing some very real commitment issues here."

"Look who's talking."

"And look who just got married." Her sister was silent for a few moments then said in an airy voice, "Married. Boy, I can't get used to saying that word, you know?"

"I know." Kyra smiled. "Oh!" She glanced at her watch. "I've got to go. I'm going to be late for work."

"You think about what I said, you hear?" Alannah said quickly.

"All right, all right. Love ya, Al."

"Love ya, Kyra."

Then Kyra immediately rushed for the door.

MICHAEL WALKED Tom Neville from the conference room, trying to hide his frustration with the irritating client behind a tight smile. "You know the changes will push the completion date back by at least a week. Maybe two."

Neville waved a hand as if he couldn't be bothered with the details. "Whatever it takes. Just so long as it's done right."

His words seemed to imply that it wouldn't have been done right by Michael otherwise. And Michael knew how nonchalant his client really was about the time frame. Which was not at all. He fully expected to get a phone call later that day telling him he expected the job to be done within three days.

"Very well, then. I think we've covered everything for now. I'll call you if I have any questions."

"I have complete faith in you and your company, Michael."

"And we're thankful for that faith."

Michael managed to maintain the thin smile until Neville called out a greeting to Phyllis, the secretary, then disappeared through the front doors. The minute he was out of sight, Michael let loose a string of curse words that got chuckles from the associates nearest to him.

He grinned and jokingly ran his hands across his forehead. "If he had stayed a second longer, I would have issued every last one of those words to his face." He clucked his tongue. "Let that be a lesson to you. Save the cursing until after the clients leave. Or else we won't have any clients."

More chuckles.

Michael found himself grinning as he strode down the hall toward Kyra's office. He stopped himself just outside with his hands on the jamb. She wasn't in there. A quick glance around found her nowhere in sight.

The secretary made a "yoo-hoo" sound that caught his attention. He looked at her. She pointed to the closed door to Janet's office, then cupped her hand over mouth and said in a stage whisper, "She's in with Janet now."

Michael squinted at the woman who had been the secretary there for longer than he cared to remember. In fact, she'd been there so long he couldn't remember who had hired her or why. But every time he or one of the guys brought up replacing her, Janet balked, claiming the strange-smelling woman was her right-hand man.

Michael stepped up to her desk. "Do you know how long they'll be?"

Phyllis's smirk made his stomach tighten. "I couldn't tell you, Mr. Romero. But she's been in there twenty minutes already."

Michael glanced at his watch. It was already past noon. The secretary never stayed over her lunch hour. He pieced that together with the knowledge that the auditor was supposed to be presenting his findings to Janet this morning and his stomach tightened even further.

He eyed Phyllis. She was fairly bursting with the desire to spread some gossip.

Pasting on the same grin he'd used with Tom Neville, he propped a hip against the desk and bent slightly, speaking in a conspiratorial manner. "What's going on?"

"Well, I really shouldn't tell you, sir."

But she would. They both knew it.

The secretary leaned forward, her face animated. "I think Janet is going to fire her."

Michael froze, his heart skipping a beat.

"And it couldn't have come soon enough, if you ask me. Prancing around in all those...slutty outfits. It's shameful."

"You can't fire someone for the way they look," Michael said, staring at the closed door.

"No, but you can fire them for embezzling."

Embezzling?

Michael pushed to his full height then stared at the secretary.

Michael strode purposely toward Janet's door. Only when he went to grasp the handle, the door swung inward and Kyra, looking as pale as he'd ever seen her, barreled straight into his chest.

"Whoa," he said, steadying her with both hands. "What's the rush?"

Behind her, Janet rose to her feet, straightening her skirt. "Miss White has just resigned from Fisher, Palmieri, Romero and Tanner."

QUIT. She had just quit her job.

Well, she hadn't merely quit her job. She'd told the chilly Janet Palmieri what she could do with it, then proceeded to give her graphic directions.

Kyra's throat felt so tight she was afraid she might choke.

She was distracted and was barely aware of brushing by Michael on her way out of the office.

Her things... She needed to clear out her things. Her ears rang with the swiftness in which everything happened. The auditor had submitted his report. The report held her accountable for the missing money. Janet said she would be contacting the proper authorities and they would probably be contacting her soon for a statement.

The authorities....

My God, was she going to be arrested? Because of a stupid accounting error?

She grabbed a box from the supply room then hurried to her office, emptying out drawers without seeing what she was taking. Then suddenly, the realization of her situation hit her, and her legs reacted the same way every other part of her body had. They gave out on her. She dropped into her chair and sat staring at the wall. A wall she'd seen nearly every day for the past four years.

"Kyra?"

She heard Michael's voice, but she couldn't seem to bring herself to respond to it.

"What happened?"

She swallowed with much difficulty then whispered, "Haven't you heard? I'm a thief."

"Did Janet fire you?"

"No. I quit."

"You shouldn't have."

Kyra frowned then slowly turned to face the man who had filled her world with pleasure such a short time ago. "What?"

"Resigned. You shouldn't have done it. Janet would have needed the approval of all the partners before she could have fired you."

She pointed toward the door. "Are you saying I should have gone through that again, this time with all four of you?" She laughed without humor. "Thanks, but no thanks." She opened the middle drawer, telling herself to take her time. The next thing she knew, Janet would be accusing her of taking office supplies. "I don't like being called a liar."

He slowly rounded her and sat on the corner of her desk. "Look at me."

She refused the request.

He curved his fingers under her chin and gently nudged her face up. "Withdraw your resignation."

"No."

His gaze roamed over her. "Why didn't you tell me things had gone this far?"

"Oh, maybe it was because I had no idea they had?"

"You had to have suspected something," he said quietly, his thumb caressing her jawline, sending little shivers over her skin despite the situation.

"I didn't. Why should I have? I hadn't done anything wrong. I have no idea who took that large petty cash withdrawal out, but it wasn't me."

She stared at him, daring him to defy her.

"Did you look into who might have done it?"

"No. I assumed it was a bank error. You know, the cashier added on an extra zero by mistake."

"And?"

"And this morning the auditor produced bank records showing the cash-out at the higher amount, given to Kyra White."

He removed his hand and clasped it with his other in his lap.

Kyra continued removing her items from her desk. Her sorry excuse for a bonsai plant that Alannah had given her during her last trip. A picture frame bearing a picture of a younger Alannah and herself. A knick-knack Michael had given her. A crystal paperweight from the partners last Christmas.

She started to put the paperweight in the box, then instead dropped it into the garbage.

"Please," she said. "I'd rather be alone now."

She glanced up to find him squinting at her in concern.

"I just need, um, a little time to adjust, you know? I feel like I've just been hit on the side of the head with a two-by-four."

"You look that way, too."

She made a face. "Thanks. That's sure to brighten my day."

He chuckled quietly. "Go home, Kyra. I'll straighten this out."

"Straighten what out? It's already done. I quit. Q-U-I-T. That's it. The end." She looked at him pointedly. "And I don't want you to do a single thing to change that."

"But—"

"What, are you hearing impaired?" she said.

Michael's eyes narrowed.

She exhaled loudly. "Sorry. I told you I'd much rather be alone right now. Either stay and risk more abuse, or leave." She tried to still her shaking hands. "Please."

"I'll see you later at your place?"

She nodded, but somehow she couldn't visualize continuing on with things as normal. Not that their relationship was normal. It was just one more anomaly heaped up on everything else.

"I'll bring B & J."

She nodded again.

Finally, Michael pushed away from the desk and started for the door. She sensed him hesitate, but she continued clearing her things out as if she didn't know he was there.

Then he was gone.

LATER THAT NIGHT, Michael climbed the steps to Kyra's apartment, bearing Chinese food and ice cream. He still couldn't figure out how everything had gotten so out of hand at the firm without his having had a clue.

After Kyra left, he'd gone into Janet's office and shut the door. But he hadn't found out anything more from her than he'd already learned from Kyra. He'd asked why he or the other partners hadn't been consulted on the matter and Janet had reminded him that she was in charge of personnel matters and she'd been the one ultimately responsible for taking care of it.

He couldn't argue that point. Annually the partners traded off on administration duties and this year Janet *was* in charge of firm matters.

All afternoon he'd mulled over the situation, trying to figure out what had happened. Just before leaving, he'd cornered Janet again and suggested that she might want to look into Phyllis Kichler as the culprit. It was no secret that Kyra and the gossipy secretary had never gotten along.

Janet indicated that she would take his suggestion under advisement but Michael got the impression that she thought the matter was closed. The firm was out three thousand dollars. Twenty-seven hundred after the three hundred that was put in the office petty cash fund. No, she didn't plan to prosecute or to try to reclaim the money, she'd said, due mostly to Michael's personal connection to Kyra.

Michael told her he planned to call the partners together to discuss the matter.

Not that he expected it to make a whole lot of difference. Yes, his actions might clear Kyra's name. But he didn't expect her to return to the firm.

He took the few remaining stairs to her apartment, feeling a hollow sensation in his chest. He liked working with Kyra. Liked seeing her at the firm every morning, sharing coffee with her, joining her for lunch, or stealing into her office for a few minutes under the guise of a professional matter to just shoot the breeze with her. Hell, he'd liked doing all that before they'd become intimately involved.

And now she would no longer be there.

He really hated that.

He juggled the items he held and raised his hand to knock.

"I wouldn't bother if I were you!"

No matter how many times Mrs. Kaminsky shouted at him, Michael didn't think he'd ever get used to the sound. He turned to look down the stairwell at her, wondering if the woman had ever been married and whether or not her husband had been deaf.

"She's not in?" he asked, frowning. He'd seen her Mustang out front. Kyra never went anywhere without her Mustang.

"Oh, she's in all right! It's you she doesn't want to see! She gave me express instructions to tell you to take a hike and not to contact her, that she'll be in touch with you when she's good and ready!"

The words came out as one long, run-on sentence, the ear-splitting volume of Mrs. K.'s voice breaking not at all.

Michael stared at her.

"I don't know what you did to her, but if you so much as harmed a hair on that girl's head, I swear I'll come after you with my broom! Now go on, get out of here before I decide to do it anyway!"

Michael raised his eyebrows and watched as she went back inside her apartment and slammed the door, practically shaking the entire building.

He swallowed hard then looked toward Kyra's

closed door. Was it true? Had Kyra requested that Mrs. K. turn him away? While the landlady was loud, he didn't know if she was capable of lying.

He didn't get it. He knew Kyra was upset. He'd be upset, too. But she'd never turned him away before. He began to walk toward the stairs, then stopped. As her friend, he would never let her off the hook that easy. Why, then, as her lover, was he running away with his tail between his legs?

Fear of rejection, he realized.

Squaring his shoulders, he turned back toward her door and knocked soundly. "Kyra? I know you're in there." He tried the handle. Locked. "Open up, Kyra. I want to talk to you."

No response.

"Okay, I *need* to talk to you. To make sure you're okay."

Still nothing. He couldn't even make out a sound in the apartment.

"Come on, Kyra—"

"Hey. Are you deaf? The girl doesn't want to see you. Now scram."

Michael started at the sound of Mrs. K.'s renewed yelling. This time she was holding the broom she had threatened him with earlier.

She started up the stairs.

Michael held up his hands the best he could considering the items he held. "Okay, okay. I'm going."

He didn't move and neither did she.

"Well?" she shouted.

He figured at this rate, he would be the one in need of a hearing aid. "Put the broom away."

"I'll do no such thing."

"Then step back from the stairs."

She squinted her eyes at him, then slowly descended the stairs.

"That's it. Keep going. Good. Now go back into your apartment."

"I'll go back into my apartment when I'm good and ready! I don't need any Johnny-come-too-often to tell me what to do!"

Michael grimaced. "Then promise me you won't hit me with that broom."

She looked at the item in question then back at him. "You don't mess with me, I won't mess with you!"

"Good."

He glanced at Kyra's still-closed door, then cautiously descended the remainder of the stairs. He began to pass Mrs. Kaminsky, then hesitated. She lifted the broom as if to whack him.

"Whoa. I'm not planning on doing anything."

"You'd better not! Because I won't hesitate to use this, you know!"

This close up, Michael winced against the onslaught of her high-decibel voice.

"Do you like Chinese?"

She stared at him as if she was reconsidering whacking him. "They're okay. Different from the Mexicans, but hey, I'm no racist."

He fought a grin. "I meant food." He held out the bags in his hands. "Here. Merry Christmas."

The old landlady didn't appear to know how to react as Michael turned and headed through the narrow hall leading to the door.

"Christmas isn't for four months!"

Michael shook his head and left.

12

THE FOLLOWING AFTERNOON, Kyra burrowed farther under the covers, ignoring Mr. Tibbs pawing at her hands and the sound of someone knocking at her front door. She knew it couldn't be Michael. Michael was at work. And Michael never put anything above work. She peeked out at the answering machine. The red digital numbers told her she had ten messages. She pulled the blanket back up, glad she'd turned the ringer off.

"Miss White! Open the door this minute! This is your landlady!"

As if she could have mistaken her for anyone else.

Kyra frowned. What was Mrs. Kaminsky doing knocking at her door?

"I know you're in there! I would have heard you had you gone anywhere!"

Kyra didn't feel like budging an inch. So she didn't. Mr. Tibbs meowed, Mrs. K. bellowed, and Kyra wished she were anyplace at that one moment but there.

If she hadn't opened the door for Michael last night, she certainly wasn't going to let her landlady in now.

Her heart gave a painful squeeze. It had been so difficult to hear him call out for her even after Mrs. K. had told him to go away. Of course the old woman had paraphrased much of what she'd said, but the message had been the same: Kyra had wanted to be left alone.

And alone she had stayed for the past twenty-four hours. Alone, holed up in her bed except for potty breaks and trips to the kitchen to feed Mr. Tibbs. Herself...well, she didn't even want to think about food, although she had sipped some water in the bathroom.

Michael would be furious with her. She knew that. But she couldn't help herself. The one thing she'd always prided herself on was her honesty. And to be unfairly accused of a crime she hadn't committed ate away at her as very few things could. Didn't he understand that?

She knew at some point very soon she'd have to drag herself out of bed and look for a new job. But right now, she could do little more than mourn the loss of her last one.

She also knew at some point she'd have to talk to Michael. But she couldn't think about that right now, either.

"You painted the stinking woodwork!"

The abnormally loud sound of Mrs. Kaminsky's voice startled Kyra straight out of bed. Gulping deep breaths of air, she stood staring at her landlady in shock. Never in the three years that she'd lived there had Mrs. K. come up the stairs, much less into her apartment. That she was standing there now, holding something in her hands, made Kyra extremely paranoid.

Mrs. Kaminsky held up a key. "I'm the landlady, remember!"

Kyra winced away from the loud sound of her voice.

"What's the matter? You been drinking, girl? Am I talking too loud for you?"

"No, I haven't been drinking," Kyra whispered,

thinking that might not be such a bad idea. "What are you doing here?"

"Your boyfriend left this for you last night. I kept it in the refrigerator waiting for you to leave for work, but when you didn't I figured something was wrong. So I decided I'd bring it up."

Kyra looked at the bags from her favorite Chinese restaurant. "I didn't go to work because I no longer have a job."

"No longer have a job! What, are you crazy, girl? Do you know what state the economy's in lately! Are you going to be able to pay your rent?"

Kyra put her hands over her ears. "Please. Could you lower it just a couple of decibels?"

Mrs. Kaminsky stared at her. "Am I talking too loud?"

"Well, yeah," Kyra said, trying to be polite, but missing the mark. By coming into her apartment, her landlady had invaded Kyra's personal space. And that meant the gloves were off. "You're about two shouts away from breaking my eardrums."

Kyra braced herself for another tirade, but was surprised when Mrs. K. pulled something out of the front of her robe. She realized it was a hearing aid. She shook it. "My sister keeps telling me I should get a new one. I tell her 'I don't need a new hearing aid. This one has worked just fine for the past ten years.'"

"I don't think it's working at all," Kyra said, crawling back into bed and covering herself with her blanket, hoping to dull the noise.

She gasped when Mrs. K. yanked the blanket back. "Is this the way you treat guests?" she shouted. "It's no wonder that the only one who comes over is that

Johnny-come-lately." She looked at the bags in her hands, then thrust them at Kyra. "Although I gotta say, a guy who brings a gal ice cream can't be all bad."

Kyra jostled the bags. Mrs. K.'s voice was lower now, almost at a normal level.

"My Herman used to bring me licorice. Cherry, not that strawberry stuff."

Kyra pulled the sheet back up to her chin and peered at the other woman. "Herman?"

"My husband. Well, late husband, anyway. Died a year or so before you moved in. Freak accident. He was painting a bridge and a pelican dive-bombed him."

Mrs. Kaminsky talked the way she shouted, in one long unbroken stream of thought. Kyra stared at her, speechless. How did one respond to the kind of information she was sharing? "Sorry." She finally managed to get something out.

"Yeah, well, it's been a few years now. We have one daughter. Penelope. She lives in Washington state. Works for some conservationist group or other. Something to do with owls. 'There's plenty of that type of work here, what with the everglades and all,' I tell her. But she don't listen to me. Calls me once a week."

Mrs. K. had a daughter?

"You remind me of her. I guess that's why I took a liking to you the first time you came by to see the apartment. 'Now here's a girl a woman can trust,' I told myself. Don't you make me out to be a liar."

Kyra felt as though she'd passed over into some parallel universe. She pinched her leg under the sheet just to make sure she wasn't dreaming.

"Now, you gonna get up or am I gonna have to start screaming again?"

Was that a twinkle in the old woman's eyes? Yes, Kyra decided, it was. And it was so unexpected, she forgot to be irritated. "I'll get up."

"Good." Mrs. Kaminsky turned from the bed and stepped toward the door. "You know it's against the lease for you to mess with anything in here."

Kyra tensed, because she'd done a whole lot of messing. From pulling up the ratty old carpeting and polishing the wood floors, to painting the walls neon colors and the woodwork white, she'd changed just about everything in the apartment.

Mrs. Kaminsky nodded. "I like it." She looked over her shoulder. "Now get yourself up and go out and find yourself another job. The first day you miss the rent, I'll boot your bony butt out of here faster than you can blink. And don't think that I won't."

Kyra scooted until her feet dangled over the side of the bed. She looked down at the bags, not doubting that all her favorites were in there. And suddenly she was ravenous.

"Mrs. K.?" she called as the woman opened the front door. "Um, where's the ice cream?"

The door slammed behind the woman's retreating back and Kyra heard her laughter in the hall. She smiled. She'd always suspected there was more to the old woman. Now that she knew that there was, she wasn't sure she liked it. Not one bit. If she wanted to waste away in her bed by herself, what business was it of anyone's? Much less Mrs. Kaminsky's?

She spotted the book she'd bought that had compelled her to change so much of her life. *Sex Kitten 101.* Yeah, right. It would have been better titled, *How to Totally Screw Up Your Life in Ten, Idiot-Proof Steps.*

She picked up the book and dropped it into the garbage can, then eyed her bed longingly.

"If you're not out of this apartment in half an hour, I'm going to come back in and get you!" Mrs. Kaminsky shouted through the door.

Kyra made a face and got out of bed, not sure what she was more afraid of: that Mrs. K. would make good on her threat or that she wouldn't....

MICHAEL PARKED HIS CAR next to Kyra's Mustang in the nightclub lot. He checked his hair in the mirror, then took a deep breath. He really couldn't say why he was so nervous. Yes, he could. He hadn't spoken to Kyra since yesterday, right after she quit the firm. He'd left no fewer than a dozen messages on her machine, and called a dozen more times above that. And at five this afternoon, she'd finally called back.

He'd been so relieved to hear her voice, he hadn't really registered what she'd said. Then she'd repeated herself. She'd landed a new job at a trendy new couture shop. She'd been shopping after a particularly depressing job interview and she and the storeowner had hit it off. And, imagine that, the store's bookkeeper had gone into labor that morning and they were in dire need of a replacement.

Kyra had wanted to celebrate. "Meet me at Lolita's after work. You know, just like old times."

Michael forced himself to get out of the car, the heat hitting him like a furnace blast. They hadn't been back to the club since they'd become intimate. And he wasn't sure he liked the idea of going back to "old times." He closed the car door, then had to open it again to get the flowers he'd picked up. They were bright and cheerful. The balloon that read Congratulations had been a little too cheerful, however, and he'd popped it once he got into the car. He figured Kyra would know what he meant.

He stepped into the dark club and gave his eyes a moment to adjust. The place was hopping with the usual after-work crowd. He squinted, looking over the tables. No Kyra. Then he spotted her. There. At the bar.

His stomach tightened, much as it always did when he saw her. But the sensation was doubly intense given the events of the past two days. She had on that clingy purple dress that hugged her in all the right places, and gained the attention of every guy in the place. He made his way in her direction, prepared to battle them all away. Then his step faltered as he noticed who was sitting at Kyra's side.

Craig Holsom.

Damn.

For a long moment Michael stood staring at the two people who had been a couple a mere ten days ago. Kyra was listening intently to something Craig was saying and he was treating her as if she were the only woman in the place. When the jerk didn't even glance at the passing waitress, Michael felt his fists clench. Then Kyra threw back her head and laughed, draping her hand easily around Craig's shoulders. Craig looked as though he wanted nothing more than to devour her.

And Michael wanted to kill him.

Instead he turned back toward the door and walked out, not particularly anxious to become ex-Jerk Number Fourteen....

KYRA LOOKED AT HER WATCH. Michael should have been there by now. She asked J.B. for the phone.

"Who are you calling?" Craig asked, leaning in a little too closely for her liking. She nudged him away.

"My date."

When she'd initially entered the club to find Craig there, she'd been psyched with the opportunity to have her ex finally see her and her new look. And oh, boy, had he reacted the way she'd hoped, instantly homing in on her even as she made it clear she was waiting for someone else and had no intention of pursuing anything further with him. But the thrill of having Craig Holsom salivate after her like a repentant dog in prime leg-humping mode started wearing very thin only two minutes into their conversation. And she wished he would disappear back into the woodwork and leave her alone.

"Boy, you work quick," Craig said, some of his old whiny self surfacing for a visit.

You have no idea, Kyra thought.

Just wait until he saw that Michael was her date.

She smiled to herself and dialed. She didn't get any answer at Michael's house, the firm, or his cell phone. That's odd. She dialed her apartment and retrieved her messages.

"Kyra, it's Michael. Can't make it tonight. Sorry. Explain later."

He had left the message five minutes ago.

Every last reason to celebrate evaporated into the liquor-saturated air. And she'd certainly had reason to celebrate.

Kyra slowly handed the phone back to J.B. then picked up her purse.

"Where are you going?" Craig asked.

She wrinkled her nose. "My date asked me to meet him somewhere else," she lied, really not sure why she had. Somehow she didn't want him to know that she'd been essentially stood up.

"Hey, I have an idea. Why don't you just stay here with me? You know, relive old times." He skimmed his finger down her bare arm. "Make some new times."

Kyra shuddered, wondering what she'd found attractive in the man looking at her as if she were on the menu. "No, thank you. I have enough memories with you to last two lifetimes."

She'd expected to feel triumphant as she walked out of the bar, head held high. Instead all she could think about was Michael, and wonder why he'd cancelled out on her.

MICHAEL DREW A LINE, then another perpendicular to it, then joined them at two spots to indicate where the new kitchen island on Neville's house design would go. He blew a long breath out and rubbed the back of his neck. He had hoped that returning to work would help chase the image of Kyra sitting with her ex-boyfriend from his mind. Instead, the silence filling the open area made it that Kyra was all he *could* think about. Not to mention the fact that he kept seeing her stretched, gloriously naked, across his worktable.

He cursed under his breath. He should have trusted his earlier instincts. He'd been afraid in the beginning that he would end up being nothing more than a rebound guy to help Kyra get past her latest breakup. And it was looking as if that's exactly what he'd ended up becoming. Worse, she might even go back to the guy she had been on the rebound from. Something that never happened before, but this seemed to be a time for firsts.

He reached for the cup of coffee he'd picked up on the way back to the office, and nearly knocked it over. He grimaced and shook droplets of the hot liquid from his hand.

"You should have read the side. Danger: Hot."

Michael looked up, his heart leaping at the prospect of seeing Kyra.

Instead, his partner Janet Palmieri stood on the other side of his drafting table, smiling at him.

What was she doing here? On his short list of people he could tolerate seeing right now, her name wasn't close to appearing. He frowned then went back to working on the blueprint. "You're here late."

"So are you."

He cleared his throat, hoping with simple body language that he could communicate that he'd rather be alone. "Neville changed the plans again."

"Shocker."

"Yeah." He erased an older line, then looked up at Janet. She seemed to have something on her mind. He would rather she didn't share it with him just then. Not after everything that had happened, precipitated by Janet's run-in with Kyra that had caused her to quit. "Have you checked out Phyllis?"

It was her turn to frown. "No."

"I see."

Michael turned back to his work. Several more moments passed, then he heard the rustling of clothing. He glanced up, expecting to see Janet going back to her office. Instead he found her undoing the buttons on her jacket and revealing the black bra she wore underneath.

Michael's eyebrows rose and he glanced to her face.

There was no way in hell she was doing what he thought she was doing. Sure, back in the beginning, he had thought Janet was attractive. He'd even had dinner with her once or twice. But over the past few years, they'd been nothing but work associates. Partners at the same firm, the only thing they had in common was the bottom line.

But right now, Janet seemed intent on showing him an entirely different bottom line. Namely hers.

She smiled. "I figured since you, you know, like to do it in the office, maybe you and I could have a go at it."

She rounded the drafting table even as Michael sat staring at her, realizing two things. First, that Janet must have been there when he and Kyra had used the table for, um, personal purposes. And second, that Janet seemed to want to reenact the scene, inserting herself into Kyra's place.

Michael tensed and told himself this wasn't happening. "Janet..."

"Shh." She shrugged out of the jacket and let the conservatively cut navy-blue material fall to the floor. "You don't have to say anything. I know this is something both of us have wanted for a very long time."

And what fantasyland did she live in?

Michael knew he should move, put some immediate distance between him and the woman advancing on him like a she-wolf. But he could do little more than stare in shock as she leaned against his drafting table in front of him, thrusting her full breasts out at him in open invitation.

Her hand disappeared behind her back then her skirt whooshed from her body, revealing a skimpy pair of panties that matched her bra.

Michael's eyes widened.

Okay, the woman was nuts. Completely, certifiably insane.

And she was kissing him.

Whoa. Something was seriously wrong here. Janet was not only kissing him, she was clawing at his shirt-front like a woman gone mad, and grinding her pelvis against his roughly.

Michael's body finally responded to the commands his brain was sending him. He simultaneously pushed her away and rolled his chair back until he had enough room to stand. "Janet, what are you doing?"

She didn't have a clue how he really felt. She stuck her finger in her mouth then dipped the dampened tip inside a bra cup. "I'm doing what I should have done years ago." She undid the clip at the nape of her neck and her hair tumbled down around her bare shoulders. "I've always had a thing for you, you know that don't you, Michael?"

He held his hand up to keep her from advancing on him again. "No, I didn't."

"Sure you did." Her hand disappeared behind her back again, then her bra loosened over her breasts. "It's just that you were always so busy taking care of Miss Scatterbrain that you didn't have a moment to act on your attraction."

Michael narrowed his eyes. Miss Scatterbrain?

"But now that she's finally gone, well, you and I can take up where we left off, can't we?"

Michael smiled, but there was absolutely no humor in the expression. "Brilliant move, that. The way you got Kyra to quit."

Janet titled her head and gave a little laugh. "Yes, I'd have to say it was a bit creative myself. I knew you'd never agree to fire her, given your...special friendship and all. So I had to find a way to make her quit."

The only place on Janet's body Michael wanted to touch was her neck. But he didn't think it would be a good idea to strangle her just then.

"Creative is exactly the word I'd have used," he said.

Her smile widened as she stepped closer to him. He grasped her arms tightly, holding her away.

He returned her smile. "And creative is exactly how I'm going to get in order to force you out of the firm."

She blinked at him. Once, twice, three times, as if incapable of understanding his words.

"Right after you admit what you did to Bryce and Harvey, and apologize to Kyra."

Janet's face reddened, but Michael suspected it had very little to do with passion. "What?" she whispered harshly.

Still holding on to one arm, he bent and retrieved her skirt and jacket, then thrust them at her. "I'd suggest you leave before you humiliate yourself even further, Janet."

PAYBACK was very definitely a bitch, Kyra decided the following day as she replaced the telephone receiver one last time, having failed in her attempt to get through to Michael. She drummed her short finger-nails against the cold plastic then looked at her watch—10:00 a.m. She knew he was at work. He had to be. Why then was he avoiding her calls? Was this his way of letting her know how it felt to be ignored? If it was, she decided she didn't like it.

Last night she'd come straight home from the club and waited for Michael to call, to explain why he had been unable to meet her as he'd promised. He never had. So she'd picked up some deli sandwiches and knocked on Mrs. Kaminsky's door. She figured her of-fer of food could do double duty. It would serve as a thank-you for lighting a fire under Kyra that morning. And to let Mrs. K. know that Kyra had gotten a new job and wouldn't be late on the rent.

Kyra absently scrunched her short hair. She didn't have to check in at her new job until after two. Which left her a whole four hours to fill. Time she was afraid she'd use to worry about her relationship with Mi-chael. And she hated to worry. Things were either one way or they were another. She'd never been particu-larly keen on waiting around to find out.

She picked up the phone and called Fisher, Palmieri, Romero and Tanner again, but rather than asking for Michael this time, she requested to speak with one of the junior associates.

There was no way in hell she was going to wait.

THE DAY was another Florida scorcher despite the breeze that kicked up off the Gulf, threatening to steal the revised blueprints out from where Michael held them against his car hood.

He squinted against the midday sun and stared at

the construction foreman. "Neville wants the island moved here," he told McFarland.

"Isn't that where it was to begin with?"

Michael grimaced and realized McFarland was right. Rather than revising the blueprint, he could have just pulled out the original one.

He ran his hand restlessly through his tousled hair. "Yeah. It is."

"This is going to cost."

Michael nodded, already well versed on how much over budget the project was going to land.

"Just so you know."

The foreman rolled up the blueprints and tucked them into his work belt, then disappeared into the large, eight-thousand-square-foot retro-style house that should have been finished a month ago.

Michael sucked in a deep breath and turned to get back into his SUV. He put a hand over his eyes as sunlight reflected off the window of an approaching car. His stomach pitched as he realized it wasn't just any other car, but Kyra's Mustang. And she was waving at him as if he'd just left her bed this morning instead of avoiding her phone calls.

Heaven help him. He could handle her so long as he didn't have to see her. She parked the Mustang and climbed out, her white flowered summer dress too short to be wearing in this kind of wind. She closed the door, then bent to retrieve something out of the back seat of the convertible. A gust caught the hem of her dress and blew it up, giving him a full view of delectable red thong underwear and her certainly more-than-perfect bottom before the material draped back down again.

Michael gulped and pulled at his suddenly too tight tie.

Kyra walked up to him, all spiky bleached-blond hair, large dark glasses and sexy playfulness.

"Hi," she said, holding a straw basket to her stomach with one hand and giving him a little wave with her other.

He squinted at her. "You know you just revealed the color of your underwear to everyone who was looking, don't you?"

"Just so long as you were looking, too, that's all that matters."

Michael's blood thrummed thickly through his veins.

Oh, boy. He was in deep trouble.

13

OKAY, this was working out better than Kyra had hoped. Not only didn't Michael seem to be mad at her, but the building site was the perfect location for what she had in mind. Positioned some fifty feet from the beach, they had a long stretch of open sand to use any way they pleased. Pleased being the key word.

"Come on. I've fixed us a picnic lunch." She slid her hand into his and tugged him toward the back of the house.

"You fixed lunch?"

"Yep. You'll be happy to know I even cooked it. No matter how much easier it would have been to pick up the food at a chicken joint." She smiled at him.

All right. Maybe there was a bit of inexplicable wariness in his eyes. But she could handle that. At least she hoped she could. It was a good sign that he was following her with little resistance.

"Here, hold this," she said, handing him the basket when they'd walked a ways down the beach, stopping in front of an area shaded by trees.

She rummaged around inside the basket until she found two beach towels. Then she began to bend over, intending to smooth them out on the white sand. Michael made a strangled sound and she quickly crouched instead. She put a hand over her eyes, judging the house to be far enough down the beach for any serious peeping.

Yes, any onlookers would be able to make out a couple on the sand, but they wouldn't be able to tell what they were doing. Not if this worked out the way she planned.

"Sit," she said, patting one of the towels.

He stood stock-still.

"What's the matter?"

He grimaced. "In case you hadn't noticed, I'm not exactly dressed for the beach."

She smiled. "That's fixable."

She stood and put the basket down next to the towels before undoing his tie and unbuttoning his shirt. He seemed oddly distracted as she tugged the shirt down his arms then folded it and the tie carefully and laid them across the basket. She bent to his shoes.

"Lift," she said.

He did. She easily removed first one shoe and sock, then the other. She considered his pants' legs, then rolled them both up to just below the knees.

She stood up to admire her handiwork and her breath seemed to be snatched straight away from her.

Michael was absolutely magnificent standing there in full sunlight, his sinfully broad chest and hard abs dark, his black hair blowing in the wind. Add the intense shadow in his eyes and you had a guy who could easily have posed for a romance book cover.

Only he was real. And he was all hers.

"Kyra," he said.

She kicked off her sandals then sat on one of the towels cross-legged. "Michael," she said in return. "I've reserved a special spot for you, right here."

He finally sat in front of her.

Good. Good. She licked her lips in anticipation and scooted a little closer.

His expression grew a little warier.

She laughed. "What is it with you today?" she asked.

"I could ask the same question of you."

She shrugged her shoulders and began rifling around in the basket for the things she wanted. Not the food. The food could wait. "I figured since you didn't want to come to celebrate with me last night, that I'd have to bring the celebration to you."

"Uh-huh. Congratulations."

She tilted her head and looked at him. "That sounds sincere."

"Yes, well, a guy has a right to be a little wary when his girlfriend avoids his calls for two days."

Warmth zinged through her at the use of the word "girlfriend." "Yes, well, I'm sorry about that."

"Uh-huh."

"What's your excuse?"

He grimaced. "What do you mean?"

"You've avoided my calls since I talked to you yesterday."

"I have not. I've been busy."

"And you're a liar."

"Maybe."

She tugged on his legs. "You don't look very comfortable. Here. Why don't you—" She pulled on his ankles until his legs were on either side of her. "There. Yes. That's better."

She scooted closer still, then stretched out her own legs so that they rested on his, their knees parallel.

She could feel the breeze on her crotch and knew

that the wind had again blown her skirt up. And if the hot look on Michael's face was any indication, he was getting more than a healthy look at the front of her thong panties. She leaned back on her arms and shimmied, giving him an even better look.

His gaze rose to hers. "Kyra? What are you doing?"

"Why, tempting your appetite, of course."

She reached inside the basket again and pulled out a square packet. "Here. A little something for you..."

AT FIRST Michael thought Kyra had given him a towel wipe. The packaging was the same size and weight. But as he tore it open, he realized it wasn't a soapy cloth at all, but a bright purple condom.

She scooted again until the front of her decadent little silk panties rested against the front of his pants. "I, um, figured this could be the appetizer," she whispered, hooking her arms around his neck.

Michael swallowed hard, instantly hard as a rock. Not that it took much. He'd been pretty far gone ever since watching her tight little butt as she'd taken the basket out of her car.

But with condom in hand, and her sweet flesh near enough for him to smell, he was dead meat.

He groaned as she pressed her full mouth against his then flicked her tongue inside. Somewhere in the depths of his mind he knew he should push her away. Demand they talk. Ask her why she'd avoided his calls. Find out what she'd been doing with Craig at the bar last night.

But as the sun beat down on top of his head, the roar of the waves a few feet away filling his ears, and with Kyra grinding tantalizingly against him seducing his senses, all he could think about was sinking into her slick, hot flesh.

He supposed that this was it. This was what happened when you let your guard down. It meant that someone now had complete control over the areas you conceded. And in Kyra's case, that meant that everything that was his was now hers. His body. His mind. His heart.

She undid his belt and the top of his pants then eased his zipper down. She freed his pulsing arousal. The sun hit the sensitive skin before Kyra wrapped her fingers around the thick shaft. Michael swallowed hard then caught her hand in his. As he hoped, she lifted her face to meet his gaze. And it was there he held her. Probing her eyes for the truth—how she felt about him, about them, about what they were about to do. In the fathomless green depths he saw desire, pure and strong. Holding her gaze captive, he rolled on the condom, using her hand and both of his to do it. Then he was pushing her skimpy panties aside and pulling her sweet flesh flush against his.

This was where he wanted to be. Always. He didn't care that they were out in the open and that the construction workers could probably see them. He fit her against him then eased her down to cover him, inch by torturous inch. She gasped but maintained eye contact, allowing him to drink in her expression of ecstasy.

He was in no hurry. And neither did Kyra seem to be. He moved slowly, their positioning preventing anything different. Slightly up, deeper into her dripping flesh, then down again.

She wrapped her legs around his waist and took him

in even deeper. He pressed his hands against her back, feeling her full body shiver though the day was hot.

Slowly...enticingly, she bore down on him. He slowly sought the front of her dress. Two tugs of the fabric freed her breasts, her nipples gloriously erect. He positioned the material so that it cupped the swells from underneath, holding her nipples upright. He bent his head to one and took his fill of the puckered flesh, tugging and sucking until Kyra's eyes finally fluttered closed and she softly cried out.

He grasped her hips and ground her against him more urgently, thinking he'd never get enough of the woman in his arms. Whether it was tomorrow or fifty years from now, he'd want her the same way as he wanted her now. Maybe even more so. He breathed, he smelled her. He closed his eyes, he saw her. He touched her, and his skin seemed to meld with hers.

Michael hadn't known he could feel this way about another person. Hadn't known you could feel this way, period. It's not that he didn't believe it when others talked about love. He just hadn't had anything to compare it to. Until now. Until Kyra.

Kyra's movements grew more restless, more frantic. He gently grasped her hips and held her still. "Shh. Not yet."

Her eyelids fluttered open and her tongue flicked out to moisten her lips.

"Here," he said, taking her arms from where they were draped around his neck. He repositioned them until they were behind her, propping her own weight against them. Then he straightened her legs out behind him and propped himself up on his own hands so that they were in pretty much in the same position, magnificently joined in the middle.

He watched her swallow as her gaze dropped down to take in the same view he enjoyed. His hard thickness half inside her slick, engorged flesh. He moved just slightly and she threw her head back and moaned.

In...and out. In...and out. Thick tension coiled in Michael's groin as he slowly made love to Kyra. And he knew that's exactly what he was doing. Making love. While he had thought that all they were having was sex before, he now knew he'd been wrong. He'd loved Kyra probably from the first moment he'd laid eyes on her. Which made being with her now that much sweeter.

Kyra's breath came in quick gasps, even though they were barely moving. He reached out and moved the hem of her dress back and away so he could watch the sculpted muscles of her abdomen. She looked down to see what he'd done, then her mouth dropped open and she moaned, her climax hitting her by surprise. Michael hit the peak at the exact same moment.

Where every orgasm he'd had up until that point had been fast and consuming, this one was slow, and painfully concentrated, seeming to go on and on, his muscles contracting in cadence with the nearby surf, shaking him down to the bone.

Kyra hit the ground before he did and clung to him as if having difficulty catching her breath. Michael put his arms around her and held tightly.

"Marry me, Michael..."

THAT WASN'T EXACTLY how Kyra had intended the words to come out. She swallowed hard, trying to regain her strength, tiny spasms still ricocheting through her body. She clamped her eyes closed. She'd intended to have wild beach sex with him, hand-feed him the food she'd made, then work her way around to proposing.

Instead she had blurted it out much the same way a man sometimes told a woman he loved her while in the mad throes of passion.

"What did you say?"

Michael's voice was barely a breath against her shoulder as he gripped her arms and gently moved her so he could look into her face.

She avoided his gaze, then smiled. "Well, that was certainly a surprise, wasn't it?" She chuckled nervously.

His eyes were filled with passion and curiosity, a mixture that made it impossible for her to look away from him.

"I mean, I planned to ask you the question...just not like that."

He didn't say anything for a long moment, merely sat there staring at her. "You're serious, aren't you?"

"As Sunday Mass."

He fell silent again, then slowly withdrew from her and plucked her from his lap. Kyra moved to fix her clothes, suddenly feeling exposed, naked.

"That sounds silly, doesn't it? My asking you to marry me?"

His expression told her that he thought she was insane.

"It's just that, I don't know, since we haven't been talking much lately, it's left me a lot of time to think. And...and..."

He narrowed his eyes.

"And you bring me ice cream."

Michael must have been very distracted because he forgot to remove the condom before zipping his pants back up.

"That's not what I meant to say. I mean, yes, you bring me ice cream. But..."

He began putting his socks back on and slid into his shirt.

She put her hand on his arm. "Please, Michael, look at me."

He did. And she almost wished he hadn't.

"You see," she said, hating the panicked sound of her voice, "when things started getting serious between us, well, I saw that as a problem. My sister, Alannah, has already pointed out to me that...well, I have commitment issues. And I've realized that I also have deep-rooted rejection issues, as well." She tried to swallow but her throat was so tight she couldn't. "I think that because of my upbringing, I have trouble opening myself up to people, trusting people..."

He was buttoning his shirt now.

"And...and..." Kyra fought to hold on to her thoughts. "That fear made me do stupid things. Like, I'd held on to a job that paid the bills because I was so damn scared of losing it that I wouldn't risk looking for anything else. Not that I was unhappy at your firm, but...well, I love my new job. I'm not just a bookkeeper. I play an important role at the store, something I didn't do at the firm. The only thing for me there was um, you, of course." She realized she was babbling, but couldn't seem to stop herself as her words came out in a rush. "And it's messed up my personal life, too. I guess I was so afraid of rejection that I'd never dare commit to any one man. Whenever it came time to go to the next level, I'd unconsciously do something to screw it up. Something that would guarantee that things wouldn't go any further." Her voice dropped. "Like what I almost did with you."

Finally he'd finished dressing and looked directly at her. The intensity of his gaze nearly knocked her over. "I love you, Kyra."

She caught her breath and her heart expanded painfully in her chest.

"I've come to accept the fact that I probably always have. From that first day we met."

"Me, too," she whispered.

He put a finger against her lips. "No. You didn't."

She opened her mouth to object, but he shook his head. "No. You've had your chance. Now it's my turn."

"But..."

"You see, I don't think that you have realized that there's always been something between us. Just like with everything else in your life, you're going with the flow. Life gives you a punch, you roll with it. Almost like you think you deserve the hit." He shook his head again. "You run into a problem at work and rather than fight it, you quit." He started to get up. "By the way, I think you'll be happy to know that Janet orchestrated the entire event."

"Janet?"

He stood to his full height and took a deep breath. "Kyra, you don't know what you want. Not really." His eyes held love as he looked at her, but they also held a level of sadness that made her stomach hurt.

"Your ex dumps you—an ex I saw you with last night—and you transform yourself. Try to make yourself into something you think he'll want."

"You saw me with Craig?" The vise around her heart tightened further. "That is definitely not what you thought it was. Yes...maybe some of my transformation was a result of his rejection. But only a small part of it, Michael. And the truth is, when he came over and sat next to me last night—while I was waiting for you, I might add—I discovered that I didn't care one way or another what he thought of me."

Michael ran his hands through his hair several times and cursed under his breath. "I spent so damn much of my own time over the past week consumed with controlling myself," he continued harshly, acting as if he hadn't heard her. "Trying not to get in too deep. Afraid that I was playing the role of the rebound relationship, the guy you go out with to help you get over your last one. I never stopped to think about you. Consider that maybe *you* weren't ready for me. For us."

"But I am," she whispered, fighting to get to her own feet.

He stared at her dubiously.

"I am!" she shouted, her ire growing. "I can't believe you're doing this!" She stalked a short ways away, then back again, kicking sand onto the towels. "For God's sake, Michael, you're treating me like a child."

He reached out a hand. She had a mind to slap it away. But instead she allowed him to cup her face with such gentleness she nearly cried. "Maybe a part of you still is a child, Kyra. Maybe that sensitive core, that place where you love, has been closed off to everything and everybody since your parents died. And now..."

She sniffled, her eyes welling with tears.

"And now, this is all so new to you that you can't possibly know what you want. And I think your brash proposal of marriage is evidence of that."

Frustration and pain swirled inside Kyra so violently she had to fight to keep her balance.

Then she lifted her bare foot and brought it down on top of his, an ineffectual gesture since he'd already put his shoes back on.

He shook his head and curved his fingers around the back of her neck. Then he kissed her.

To Kyra, it felt very much like goodbye....

14

TWO WEEKS LATER, Michael came to realize one important thing—he was a pompous ass. And the results of that pompousness were something he had to deal with from the time he woke up in the morning, until he went to bed at night.

But he still thought he was right.

Kyra couldn't possibly know what she wanted. She'd dyed her hair from brown to blond and had seemed determined to play the part all the way through. She'd been like a teenager with her first taste of freedom. That eighteen-year-old that married right out of high school because, well, it seemed like the thing to do at the time.

But Michael knew that those types of relationships very rarely made it. He knew friends from college who were divorced already, for God's sake, and some of them had already moved on to marriage number two.

The only problem was, that every now and again, he wondered if it was really Kyra who didn't know what she wanted, or if *he* was the one who had run screaming in the other direction for *fear* that Kyra didn't know what she wanted.

Or plain fear, period.

Michael idly ran his hands through his hair, the memory of the look on Kyra's face when he'd turned down her proposal twisting his gut. She'd put everything on the line. Everything that was important to her. And even when he began his arrogant speech, questioning her sincerity, she hadn't retreated. She'd plowed ahead, determined to win him over. And he'd turned her away.

Damn, damn, damn.

It wasn't often that Michael sat and thought about his life. He'd spent so much time merely living it, working toward his professional goals, ignoring his personal needs, that the way of life was pretty much par for the course for him. He'd really never thought about marriage and family the way a lot of guys did. Part of the reason stemmed from his own struggle to identify himself as a person. As just Michael Romero. Not Michael Romero, architect. Or Michael Romero of mixed Latino heritage.

Another undeniable part of his problem grew from his need for absolute control. In his professional life, control was key. But it wasn't until Kyra had made him lose control that he'd realized he'd tried to exact that same control in his personal life.

He switched off the lamp above his drafting table and sighed. It was after six and he was the only person left at the firm. Of this, he was absolutely certain. He'd met with his other partners the day after Janet's sick seduction scene and shameless admission and they'd voted unanimously that she had to sell her shares back to them at market value.

But Janet's wasn't the only office left empty. Kyra's was, too. And soon the secretary that Janet had barred any of them from firing would also be leaving. Not because they'd let her go, but because she was following Janet wherever she was going.

Good riddance.

Michael rubbed his face with his hands and sighed. He really should get something to eat. At someplace he and Kyra had never gone. The problem with that was that they'd tried nearly every restaurant within a twenty-mile radius, leaving him with very few options.

The phone rang, jarring him from his thoughts. After five o'clock the caller was given the option of punching in the extension number to leave a specific message for the person they were calling. But rather than allowing the call to go to voice mail, Michael plucked up the receiver. If he hoped it was Kyra, he wasn't telling.

"Hello?"

Tom Neville's voice rang out loud and clear. "Michael, I'm so glad I caught you."

Michael propped his elbow against his table and rubbed his temples.

"Samantha and I have changed our minds again. This time it's the master bath. What we'd like you to do—"

Michael sat staring blindly at the plans in front of him and only half listened to the imprudent man on the other end of the line. The master bathroom was done, but that didn't matter. "Rip it all out and start again," Tom said. They wanted the tub on the other side. And they'd changed their minds on the color scheme. They'd have to take the pale pink porcelain tub back in exchange for an emerald-green one. Oh, and the sink, too.

The mention of the color made Michael think of Kyra's eyes. Wide and expressive and reflecting her every emotion. Even in bed. Especially in bed.

Then he remembered the pain they'd held when he'd effectively called her an idiot. He cringed.

"You got all that?"

Michael tuned back in on the conversation. "Yes. Yes, I got it."

"Are you sure? I want you to take down every word I'm saying. Because we need to get it right this time."

Michael's jaw tightened. "There's nothing wrong with it now."

Neville fell silent on the other end of the line.

Michael had never questioned a client before. He'd always just...gone with the flow.

He recognized the words he'd told Kyra on the beach and cringed again.

"Look, Michael, I know this is last minute and that the house is scheduled to be done tomorrow, but this is something Sam and I really want."

"Just like the twenty other changes." He pulled on the edge of the blueprints in front of him and began rolling them up. "That's it, Tom. No more changes."

"Oh."

"If you decide you want anything more done, you're going to have to contact another firm."

And with that, Michael hung up.

He sighed and pressed his fingertips tightly against his closed eyelids to ward off the headache building there. What had he done? Neville had enough friends to keep the firm busy for the next fifty years. Yet he'd essentially just told the idiot to get lost.

The phone rang again. He stared at it, weighing his options. This could be the point where he apologized and agreed to do whatever Neville wanted him to. It was, after all, his money.

Yes, but it was Michael's life.

He answered the phone. "Look, Tom, nothing you could say is going to change my mind—"

"Michael?"

Oh, God.

It was Kyra.

Michael's heart beat so loudly he was certain she could hear it.

He hadn't heard from her in two weeks. And he hadn't tried to call her, either. Well, maybe there was that one time when he'd called and hung up when she answered, but that didn't count because she didn't have Caller ID.

"Kyra?" he said, thinking he had said it before, but he must not have.

"Hi."

"Hi, yourself."

There was the sound of a package being opened on the other end of the phone. "I was just wondering what you had on tap for dinner tonight."

Michael's brows pulled together. She was acting as though they'd just spoken yesterday.

"I was thinking about getting some BBQ."

"Good. I'm making spaghetti."

He smiled, his every muscle relaxing. Oh, how he'd missed her. Not just her lush body but her friendship. She could make him laugh in a way no one else ever would.

"With garlic bread?"

"With garlic bread."

"Good."

He went silent, not quite knowing what to say. Things between them...well, they hadn't exactly ended well. So what did this phone call mean? Was it what his contemporaries called a booty call? When a woman or a man called an ex out of the blue for a hot sexual fling for the night?

"I know what you're thinking," Kyra said. "You're wondering what this means, my calling you like this."

"Um, yeah. Something like that."

She didn't say anything for a long moment. "Then is it enough to say that I miss my best friend?"

No, it wasn't. He wanted to hear much more. But that was a start. "Same here."

"Good. Then I'll see you in twenty minutes?"

"Yes, twenty."

THE OLD KYRA would have given up the moment Michael walked away from her on that damn beach two weeks ago. And, in a sense, she supposed she had. For a while, anyway. Two long, agonizing weeks to be exact. Fourteen days in which she operated on automatic pilot, going to work at her new job, returning home, feeding Mr. T., feeding herself, reading, then going to bed early. If her movements seemed a bit lethargic, well that was to be expected, wasn't it? After all, it wasn't every day that a girl asked a guy to marry her only to be told she was too flighty to know what she wanted.

Then this morning, she'd woken up and lain in bed, staring at the ceiling, a restless energy reverberating through her body, a frustration that refused to be ignored. Then without knowing where it came from, she let out a yell that sent Mr. Tibbs shooting from the bed and Mrs. Kaminsky pounding on her ceiling.

She'd had it. She'd given the old Kyra two full weeks

to convince her that this is the way she should handle things. And the little wimp had cried and moped until she wanted to scream.

In fact, she had screamed.

But the new Kyra, the Kyra she had come to know under the guise of bleached-blond hair and take-charge energy, emerged triumphant, sticking her tongue out at the person she used to be, giving herself what essentially amounted to a swift kick in the butt. She wasn't anywhere near giving up. Not without presenting at least a token fight, anyway. Forget token. She was declaring all-out war.

Okay, so Michael had accused her of hiding behind her new looks. She twisted her lips and realized for the first time that that's exactly what *he* had done, the hypocrite. He saw blond hair and short skirts and automatically judged her incapable of making a serious decision. Because, of course, all that peroxide could have short-circuited a few important brain cells.

That was supposed to be her excuse. What was his?

He was scared spitless, she realized.

And she wasn't? But at least she didn't look right into his eyes and call him a yellow-bellied coward.

If he thought he was scared now, just wait until she got through with him tonight.

With her new mind-set, it had taken her no time at all to formulate a plan that would haul him back into her life. Whether it would be as her friend or her lover, she didn't know. What she did know was that she wanted the whole nine yards. And she was not going to stop until she got it.

MICHAEL CLIMBED THE STEPS to Kyra's apartment quietly, afraid that, at any moment, Mrs. Kaminsky would open her door and start chasing him with a broom. He stood on the second-floor landing and took a deep breath. He hadn't been here in so long that his chest felt tight. In all honesty, he didn't know what to expect. A part of him wanted things between him and Kyra to go back to the safety of their friendship. But most of him wanted to walk in that apartment, toss her over his shoulder, then carry her back to her bedroom.

Every night, all night, he swore he could feel Kyra's presence next to him. Inside him. As if she were there, just under his skin. And the passage of time had done nothing to eliminate that sensation.

He heard a creak on the floorboards and looked down the stairs to find Mrs. Kaminsky looking up at him, her arms crossed over her bathrobe and...was that a smile on her craggy face? Yes, he believed it was.

"Well?" she asked in a voice he was unfamiliar with. A normal voice at a human decibel level. "What are you waiting for? Knock on the door."

Uh-oh. Something was very definitely wrong if Mrs. K. was being nice to him. He stared at Kyra's closed door, terrified of what he was leaving himself open for. And more than a little excited to find out.

He knocked on the door once. Then again.

Finally it opened.

And he found himself staring at the Kyra he once knew. The Kyra he'd been friends with for four years.

A sigh of relief filled his cheeks and he smiled at her as he took her in.

Her spiky blond hair was once again brown and softly styled. Her calf-length skirt and boxy white blouse covered nearly every inch of skin and was reassuringly unrevealing.

"Hi," she said, motioning for him to come in.

"Hi, yourself." He stepped inside and she closed the door behind him.

"You look—" He gestured to her appearance. "You look more like the woman I used to know."

Something decidedly decadent entered her expression. "Yeah, she looks familiar to me, too."

Michael seemed incapable of movement. While the outer trappings had changed, the core woman was exactly the same. Her mouth with or without lip gloss was infinitely kissable. And he discovered that the clothes made his palms itch with the desire to peel them away and explore the treasures hidden underneath.

Kyra's lips twisted as if she'd read his thoughts.

Michael cleared his throat and held up a six-pack of beer and a bottle of Chianti. "I, um, didn't know which one you would want, so I brought both."

She reached for the beer. "Why don't you put the wine in to chill? Maybe we'll have some later." She led the way into the kitchen and put the six-pack on the small bistro-type table that she'd set for dinner. He put the wine in the refrigerator then closed the door, eyeing a bag on the counter. It held a stack of videos. New releases that he hadn't seen, mainly because he hadn't had his viewing buddy.

He heard a sound behind him. His brows pulled together. It was almost like a low humming. Or maybe a purring. He turned around, looking for the cat.

Kyra cleared her throat. "Um, why don't you have a seat? The garlic bread will just be a few more minutes."

"Okay."

She cracked open two beers and handed him one after he'd sat down. "So how's everything going at the firm? I gathered from the way you answered the phone that you're still having problems with Neville?"

He grimaced and took a slug of the cold brew. "Not anymore. I told him to screw off."

Kyra's eyes widened. She wasn't wearing the thick charcoal she'd taken to applying, but the movement reminded him of the way they looked when she had. "You're kidding?"

"Well, maybe I didn't use those exact words, but I did tell him that I wouldn't be making any more changes."

Her smile tripped a trigger low in his stomach. "Good for you." She held out her bottle. He clinked his against it. "Here's to taking charge."

Michael had the bottle halfway to his lips, then froze. It struck him that that's what the blond Kyra would have said. The brunette Kyra would have asked him if he thought it was a good business move, not giving the customer what he wanted.

"Something wrong?" she asked, moving a bowl of salad from the counter to the table.

"Wrong? Um, no. No, everything's fine."

And it was.

Wasn't it?

Kyra had come to her senses and had gone back to being herself. That certainly counted for something.

So what if he found himself looking for those short skirts and clingy tops? And leaning just so, trying to get a peek inside the traditional slit in her skirt when she walked? This is what he'd wanted all along, wasn't it? The other Kyra had stolen away too much of his control. Made it impossible to think straight, not to mention made him crazy with lust.

He shifted in his chair, realizing that his reaction to her, regardless of how she dressed, was just as powerful.

He grimaced. Did he have a hard-on? He swallowed some more beer and grinned at Kyra's questioning gaze. Oh, yeah. He had a whopper of a hard-on.

Aw, hell...

He rubbed his temples then homed in on that strange humming sound again. He looked around. "Is Tibbs around somewhere?"

"Tibbs?"

The sound had stopped. He waved his hand. "Never mind."

He glanced into his lap, hoping that evidence of his condition wasn't too obvious. He didn't want Kyra to get the wrong idea. If she wanted to go back to being just friends, then he'd honor her wishes.

Or try his damnedest anyway.

"Ready," Kyra said in a low, sultry voice that nearly sent him catapulting from the chair.

She put the garlic bread down in the middle of the table then took off her oven mitt. "You're wound up tighter than a drum. What's the matter?" she asked, her face all innocence.

Michael squinted at her, his suspicions raised. "Nothing. I just, um, spilled a little bit of beer on my pants."

"Let me get a towel."

Michael made sure to spill some of the beer, just a drop, to make good on his story and held out his hand for the towel. Instead Kyra crouched next to him and began blotting at the spot herself.

It took herculean effort not to groan.

"Um, that's enough," he said, quickly taking the towel from her hands.

She blinked up into his face, a sexy, knowing expression in her green, green eyes.

"Okay. I'll just get the spaghetti." She got up, allowing him a generous flash of leg as she did so. The air-conditioning was on, but Michael discovered he'd broken out in a sweat.

"Look, Kyra, I..."

She put his plate down in front of him. "Yes?"

She put her own plate down and sat across from him.

"I...well, I just wanted to apologize, you know, for saying what I did on the beach...."

She forked a meatball with gusto and Michael found himself wincing. "Why? You were right. I was acting like a child." She made a sound of disbelief. "I'm horrified just remembering what I did. Dressing like that. Asking you...well, you know."

Well...you know? She'd asked him to marry her. Had she really gotten over him that easily?

He turned his fork in his spaghetti. "Right or wrong, it was cruel for me to say it."

She chewed slowly, her gaze glued to his face.

He coughed. "Arrogant. Pompous."

"Ass."

He raised an eyebrow.

She smiled. "Just finishing the sentence. You know, pompous ass." She took a sip of beer, fastening her lips seductively around the opening. Michael found himself swallowing hard. "Not that I'm calling you one or anything."

"Of course not."

He put his mind to the task of eating his dinner, and getting his thoughts well away from areas it was better for him not to think about. Such as the way her slender throat contracted when she swallowed. Or the unconscious way she stroked her beer bottle as if she were stroking him.

The low hum sounded again. He jerked his gaze from his plate and looked to where Kyra was taking a bite of pasta. She smiled at him.

"What?"

He shook his head and grimaced. He could have sworn the sound came from her direction. "Do you have Mr. Tibbs on your lap?"

She laughed. "No. What would make you think that?"

Okay, he was losing it.

"Nothing."

She pointed her fork toward his plate. "How is it?"

"Good. It's good. Thanks for having me."

If only he didn't want to have *her* right then. Preferably stretched across the small table, the baggy top and long skirt gone.

He cleared his throat. "You know, I do have to say that I...well, I miss the blond Kyra a little," he said, half to himself.

"Whatever for? She was a royal pain in the butt."

She was the best thing that had ever happened to them both, he realized. "No. I wouldn't say that."

"But you did. Back on the beach. Remember?"

"No. I said that perhaps she, I mean the transformation, had maybe messed up your wiring, that's all." He rubbed the back of his neck. Were they really talking as if there were two Kyras? The one in front of him who was polite and nice and easy to talk to and the one that added sizzle to a room just by entering it?

He shook his head.

"What do you miss about her?"

"Huh?" Michael fought to regain his composure. Not a displayed breast anywhere and he was still so hard it hurt. "What do I miss about her?"

"I thought that was my question."

"Um," he said, stalling. "Well, I guess I miss her..." What? Her forwardness? Her daring? Her making decisions for him because he was too much of a damn coward to make them for himself?

He realized it was all of the above.

"Everything," he said, meeting Kyra's gaze.

"Everything?"

He grinned, seeing the spark of challenge in her eyes. "Yes. Everything. I miss touching her. Kissing her."

"Mmm, hmm."

He noticed she'd stopped eating and was slowly wiping her mouth with a paper napkin.

His stomach tightened further.

"I miss tasting her. Hearing her cry out my name when she comes." His voice grew lower and lower until he was almost whispering.

"What else?" Kyra whispered back, her pupils dilating until they nearly took over the green of her eyes.

"I miss the way she makes me feel," he said. "Hell, Kyra, I miss you, period." He swallowed with difficulty. "Because regardless of the outer packaging, it's you we're talking about here, isn't it? Brown hair, blond. Short skirts, long. It doesn't matter. It's you I miss. Completely."

There it was. That sound again.

Kyra got up from the table and slowly rounded it. "And she misses you."

She?

He found out exactly who Kyra was talking about as she worked her buttons, revealing the clingy white tank top she wore underneath. Next came the long skirt, uncovering the tight black leather skirt that hugged her slender hips and shapely bottom.

Michael's breath caught in his throat as he realized he'd been tricked. Kyra hadn't changed. She'd merely made him think she had.

He groaned and pulled her to him.

"You evil, evil woman."

She laughed huskily, running her fingers through his hair, then trailing them down his shirtfront to his pants. She lifted an eyebrow as she found his thick erection and gave an experimental squeeze. "You stupid, stupid man."

And he'd definitely been that. And much much more.

"You know, beauty, no matter how it's displayed, is only skin-deep. But it wasn't until I started displaying that skin, my skin, that I unearthed the woman lurking underneath all those layers of clothing and mental barriers. And, let's face it. You didn't have a clue what to do with me." She shrugged her shoulders and straddled him, putting her lusciously displayed breasts at mouth level. "So I figured if I changed that wrapping just a bit, put the whole outer transformation issue aside, that you'd come to know what I do." Her voice dropped to a whisper. "Namely, that you love me."

And oh, boy, did he.

"And that I love you."

Michael eyed her breasts, her words zinging in his brain, but his groin tempting him to do more than think. So he did the only natural thing. He fastened his mouth over her right breast through the material of her tank top, creating a large wet spot around her jutting nipple. She gasped and held him there.

Michael had no idea how he'd ever thought he could live without the woman in his lap. She was everything he'd ever hoped for and more. And, it seemed, she knew what he wanted better than he did.

Which could only mean that she knew her own mind, as well.

Their time apart, combined with his pent-up frustration, and his overwhelming feelings for her compelled him to do something he had never considering doing, but felt oh, so right doing now.

He caught her head in his hands and held her still, his gaze focusing on her beautiful face. "I know you asked me, and I'm sorry I didn't think you were serious. Or maybe I was just too much of a coward to think differently, but..." He kissed her languidly, sliding his tongue against hers, not emerging again until he got a good long taste of the woman he loved. "Marry me, Kyra." He kissed her again. "Rock my world not just tonight. But forever."

She stared at him long and hard, passion and suspicion in her eyes. "That's not why I asked you here, Michael."

"No, I know it's not." He dropped his hands down

over her back then squeezed her soft bottom, pressing her against his arousal. "But humor me anyway."

"Then, no," she said, a mile-wide smile playing on her full, luscious lips.

He grinned back at her. "No?"

He slid a hand under the slick material of her leather skirt pressing his thumb against her tight flesh. She shivered all over.

"Do we want to try that again?"

She restlessly licked her lips. Michael heard that sound again, then realized it had been coming from her all along. A cross between a purring cat and a needy, sexy woman. A wildcat that he had made the mistake of trying to stick back into the bag.

"Let's try this again," he murmured, slipping a finger inside the damp crotch of her panties and stroking her. "Marry me, Kyra."

He thrust his finger deep into her hot, tight flesh and she moaned. "Oh, yes. Michael. Yes, yes, yes."

Michael got up from the chair, taking her with him. He was going to do what he wanted the instant he first entered the apartment. "That's more like it," he said, then slammed the bedroom door behind them....

_____Epilogue_____

Three months later...

WELL, _that certainly went well._

Michael closed the door after his parents and Mrs. Kaminsky and turned to face his wife.

His wife. As his gaze lingered on Kyra where she was loading the dishwasher after the long meal they'd just served, he thought the word woefully inadequate. She was his lover. His best friend. His future. _His wife._

"Do you think your parents have forgiven me yet?" Kyra asked.

"For what?"

She wiggled her hips, making the leopard print on her short skirt slide against her rounded bottom. "Well, for dragging you to the justice of the peace and making you marry me without anyone knowing about it, of course."

"Oh, that."

Michael chuckled as he collected the empty coffee cups from the dining room table and put them on the counter next to Kyra.

"As I recall, there wasn't any dragging involved."

Ah, his parents. He remembered a time when he'd been afraid of what they'd make of Kyra. Ironic, then, that Kyra seemed to get along better with them than he ever had. Not only that, but she made him see them in a whole different light. No longer did he feel he had to play some sort of good-boy role. Instead he was now able to sit back and enjoy their company. And he discovered he not only liked them, but that they liked him. Him. Not who he had been trying to be to please them. Not the well-mannered son who came to dinner the last Sunday of every month armed with good manners, but the man who had finally broken out of his shell and disagreed with them more than he agreed. And in doing so, had finally managed to find the person who had been hiding inside.

His grin widened. All that without a bottle of hair dye. He leaned against Kyra's side and kissed her exposed neck, eyeing the blond strands that still rested against the nape.

Of course, it didn't hurt that he had the whole grandchild issue going in his favor, either, but he wouldn't think about that right now.

"I think Mrs. Kaminsky warmed up there halfway though dinner," Kyra said, putting the last of the cups in the dishwasher, then drying her hands.

Michael chuckled. "Yes. I suppose you could say her telling my parents about all the racket we make up here and how you and she made a deal that she would shut off her hearing aid every night at ten o'clock was a form of warming up."

Kyra snaked her arms around his neck and laughed against his chest. "Oh, God. I thought I was going to die when she said that."

"Did you notice the way my dad kept looking at his watch after that?" He stroked her back. "Of course, both my parents are probably hoping that our noisy activities will produce a grandchild."

"Only your parents?" She looked up at him, her eyes smiling. "Right after you moved in here, Mrs. K. sent away for a crocheting kit. She's already half done with a hideous florescent-yellow baby blanket."

Michael clucked his tongue. "I still can't believe I let you talk me into moving in here with you."

Kyra tilted her head to the side and swiveled her hips slightly. "I didn't talk you into anything. I merely suggested that since I'd already done so much to the place, and since your place no longer suited even you, that this would be a better place to live."

"Until we find something else we both like," he added.

"Hmm." She lowered her head to the collar of his shirt and pressed a hot kiss there.

Michael closed his eyes and rubbed his chin against the top of her spiky hair. Kyra's apartment had emerged the only viable choice. She was right. His condo had never really suited him. While this place...this place was bound to make anyone reconsider their lives with its bright, neon colors and va-va-voom decor.

"This being married definitely has its benefits, don't you think?" Kyra whispered, dragging her tongue along his jawline then blowing on the damp area.

Two brief knocks sounded from the downstairs apartment. "Oh, yeah."

Kyra glanced at the wall clock. "Is it ten already?"

He swept her up into his arms and began carrying her to the bedroom. "Uh-huh."

But rather than taking Kyra to the bed, he kicked open the bathroom door instead.

"What are you doing?" she whispered, her husky laughter filling his ears.

"Considering how hot you made me throughout dinner with your under-the-table activities," he said, glancing at her feet, "I thought we both might need a shower first."

He watched her quickly shimmy out of her clothes and within moments she was standing gloriously bare in front of him.

"You know, there is such a thing as playing hard to get."

She smiled. "Are you kidding? You *and* the shower massager together? You're talking fantasy material here." She ripped open the shower curtain. "Get in there, Mr. Romero."

He did as she asked, then held out his hand to help her in after him. "Whatever you say, Mrs. Romero."

"Mmm," Kyra said, making that low purring sound deep in her throat....

Blaze™

The Trueblood, Texas
tradition continues in...

HARLEQUIN® *Blaze*™

TRULY, MADLY, DEEPLY
by Vicki Lewis Thompson
August 2002

Ten years ago, Dustin Ramsey and Erica Mann shared their first
sexual experience. It was a disaster. Now Dustin's determined to
find—and seduce—Erica again, to prove to her, and himself, that
he can do better. Much, *much* better. Only, little does he guess
that Erica's got the same agenda....

Don't miss Blaze's next two sizzling Trueblood tales:

EVERY MOVE YOU MAKE by Tori Carrington
September 2002
&
LOVE ON THE ROCKS by Debbi Rawlins
October 2002

Available wherever Harlequin books are sold.

TRUEBLOOD, TEXAS

HARLEQUIN®
Makes any time special®

More fabulous reading from
the Queen of Sizzle!

LORI
FOSTER

with

*Forever
and Always*

Back by popular demand are the scintillating stories of
Gabe and Jordan Buckhorn. They're gorgeous, sexy
and single…at least for now!

Available wherever books are sold—September 2002.

And look for Lori's *brand-new* single title,
CASEY in early 2003

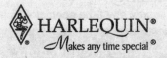

eHARLEQUIN.com

| community | membership |

buy books | authors | online reads | magazine | learn to write

Visit eHarlequin.com to discover your one-stop
shop for romance:

buy books

♥ Choose from an extensive selection of Harlequin,
Silhouette, MIRA and Steeple Hill books.

♥ Enjoy top Harlequin authors and *New York Times*
bestselling authors in Other Romances: Nora Roberts,
Jayne Ann Krentz, Danielle Steel and more!

♥ Check out our deal-of-the-week specially discounted
books at up to 30% off!

♥ Save in our Bargain Outlet: hard-to-find books at great
prices! Get 35% off your favorite books!

♥ Take advantage of our low-cost flat-rate shipping on all
the books you want.

♥ Learn how to get FREE Internet-exclusive books.

♥ In our Authors area find the currently available titles of
all the best writers.

♥ Get a sneak peek at the great reads for the next
three months.

♥ Post your personal book recommendation online!

♥ Keep up with all your favorite miniseries.

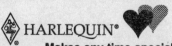

HARLEQUIN®

Makes any time special®—online...

Visit us at
www.eHarlequin.com

HINTBB

HARLEQUIN® *Blaze*™

**The Masterson brothers—Zane and Grey.
Both gorgeous, both oh-so-sexy.
*Identical?***

Natural-born lady-killers Zane and Grey Masterson are
notorious among the female population of New Orleans
for their "love 'em and leave 'em smiling" attitudes.
But what happens when they decide to switch places—
and each brother finds himself in an intimate struggle
with the one woman he can't resist...?

Find out in...

DOUBLE THE PLEASURE by Julie Elizabeth Leto
&
DOUBLE THE THRILL by Susan Kearney

*Both books available in August 2002,
wherever Harlequin books are sold.*

**When these two guys meet their match,
the results are just two sexy!**

HARLEQUIN®
Makes any time special ®